THE VANISHING BALLERINA

JAMESON KEYS

A Bobby Bocchini Mystery

Print ISBN: 979-8-35093-5-707
eBook ISBN: 979-8-35093-5-714

For Caroline and Connor. You are my heart and my soul. My very reason for being.

In memory of my mother Marian. I miss you every day.

In memory of Charles and Marian Berryhill. Great teachers, a greater love story.

TABLE OF CONTENTS

PROLOGUE

(New York City, 2014)

T he girl jumped as her mobile phone buzzed. It was her mother yet again.

"Hello, Mommy."

"Jessica, my meeting is running longer than expected. Call your father and have him pick you up at the studio. Do you understand?"

"Yes, Mommy," she replied. "I will, I promise."

Her mother hung up.

She was unsure why her mother did not call her dad directly. Jessica noticed the growing tension between her parents. She worried it was her fault again. The day was dragging on. She already spent seven hours at school and an hour in ballet class with two hours of homework overseen by her father, yet to come. Jessica longed for a little personal time. She just needed twenty minutes to herself. She sometimes imagined herself as a beautiful bird that could just rise high above the city and fly away. When Jessica grew up, she dreamed of being a filmmaker or detective. Why not both? She pondered. Her mother naturally had other ideas. According to her, Jessica would be an engineer, or better yet, a doctor. That would make her mother happy indeed. However, that was not what Jessica wanted. Jessica was, by any measure, exceptionally bright. Besides her normal coursework, Jessica enrolled in advanced classes years above her grade level. Her test scores were off the charts, especially in mathematics. She loved puzzles and chess, anything that she could solve. It is just five blocks to Daddy's office, she thought. I am not a baby. I will just turn up. Dad will say, "Jessica, what a big girl you have become!" Jessica loved her mother naturally, but she adored her father. She told her ballet instructor a little fib—that her dad was waiting for her outside.

The teacher bent down, zipped her coat, and patted her on the head. "Ok, Jess, hurry to the car."

Jessica was incredibly mature for her age. She always paid meticulous attention to instruction and was the first to master additional steps or techniques. When she performed, she was, in a word, flawless. The teacher trusted implicitly that her father was indeed just outside in the car. The instructor's next class was starting, and two fussy little girls were squabbling about their spot at the bar. Jessica took out her phone. Her father, a successful hedge fund manager, bought her an expensive one for Christmas as a special gift. He did so despite his wife's objections. He also included an assortment of lenses that snapped on the outside of the phone, allowing her to use the camera to indulge her love of photography and for making her little movies, or short features, as she called them. Jessica clipped on one of the fisheye lenses and walked onto the sidewalk.

It was a cold, windy day in the city. She pulled her cap down to cover her ears and adjusted her scarf around her neck. Jessica could smell one of the food trucks parked just down the street. Her stomach involuntarily growled, but she ignored it. Jessica scanned the streets and people of New York to create an "establishing shot." She noticed a cab driver yelling at another cab driver. Also, a woman had just broken off her heel in a steam grate. Jessica chuckled. It was at that point she caught sight of him, a familiar face she had seen many times before. He wandered the street close to her ballet studio and in the restaurant that she and her dad sometimes ate at on Saturdays for pancakes. The man always looked so sad. She wondered why.

Jessica recently checked out *The Complete Sherlock Holmes, Volume One,* by Sir Arthur Conan Doyle at the public library near her house. The opposite of light reading, especially for a seven-year-old, the alien landscape of Victorian England mesmerized her. Sherlock Holmes inspired her to see the things in the world that others missed. Take the sad man, who was he and why did he meander the streets? Recently she created a detective case log with notes on the "sad man." He continued down the alley across the street. I wonder where he goes. She glanced at the clock on her phone. Jessica had a brief window to find out before heading to her father's office. A good detective needs to be skilled in the art of surveillance, she thought. I might learn what makes him so sad. She hesitated momentarily, weighing her options, but then pressed on. Carefully, she crossed the street at the light, filming as she walked. Jessica crept down the alley and simply vanished.

ONE:

A MYSTERIOUS GENTLEMAN

"**C**an I get you more coffee, Bobby?" Tina asked. She was a twenty-some-thing purple-haired server with a neck tattoo, a nose ring, and an exces-sive amount of eye shadow. Bobby was meeting with a potential client, ten minutes late. Bobby earned his livelihood as a private investigator, a part-time Uber driver, and whatever else, helped him cover his alimony payment and other expenses. "No thanks, Tina. All good here." It was sometimes hard for him to fathom how he had arrived at this point in his life.

Not so long ago, Bobby was a Marine serving in operations in Desert Shield and Storm. It was part of his overall plan. In 1992, Bobby completed his commitment to the Corps. After his service, he fulfilled a lifelong dream by taking the entrance exam to become a police officer in the Big Apple. He entered the police academy, and shortly after became one of New York City's finest. He had nine years on the job on September 11th, 2001. People assume they comprehend the mayhem of that day. However, mere words cannot describe the unimaginable horror of it all. He thought it was Armageddon, the end of the world. Bobby had just started his shift when the first call came in. A plane had crashed into the World Trade Center.

"How shitty of a pilot do you have to be to hit that?" Sal Mancuso, his Captain, said. Bobby had just received a promotion to detective third grade by that point. "It's only the biggest freaking building in the world!" Sal, Bobby, and senior detectives Reynolds and Baker watched the news of the plane crashing into the World Trade Center on the break room TV. A subsequent report speculated that it was a Boeing 757.

"A commercial jet?" Bobby asked. "That is impossible." Within minutes, all four men were running to their vehicles. The fires had already trapped many people on the higher floors. When they arrived, it was like a war zone, with people running, crying, screaming. Papers from the offices above fell like snowflakes, and a thick acrid smoke filled the air. Bobby pulled on his police windbreaker and reported his readiness to the operations coordinator. "Chief, where do you need us?" Sal remained with operations as he just had a knee replacement and could not climb that many stairs.

The rest of the team ascended the stairs as a group. The goal was the 60th floor to help the injured down. At that very moment, the second plane slammed into the south tower. The dust and smoke were already thick. Bobby was choking on the toxic mixture. He found a black bandana in his pocket, and he poured water on it and wrapped it around his face like an old western bandit. He was operating on sheer adrenaline.

They completed the first round-trip. There was no time to waste; Bobby paused, exhausted from the exertion of the climb. As he looked up, the carnage intensified. Dear God, he thought. People trapped above the fire were jumping to avoid being burned alive. Bobby was a man grounded in his faith and the Catholic Church. Bobby would face many tests of his faith in the coming days. He pressed on.

Bobby was on his way down from the 45th floor when the Tower fell. He heard a rumble like distant thunder, and then everything turned black. Bobby carried a petite accountant from Newark with a broken leg from the initial attack. On any other day, Bobby was a formidable guy, six foot four inches and 220 pounds of Italian tank. On that day, he was tossed around like a tissue in a tornado. He somehow hung on to Doris Levine, maybe gripping her a little too tight. In fact, he dislocated her arm in the fall. Miraculously, they both survived the initial plunge into darkness.

Detectives Reynolds and Baker were not as lucky. Weeks later, volunteers would find their bodies. Bobby awoke in total darkness, in tremendous pain, but alive. He could not feel his left leg and assumed he had lost it in the collapse. Finding his Maglite in his pocket, he saw that his leg was still there, just pinned behind him. It was under hundreds, if not thousands, of pounds of debris. He tried his best to control his breathing and his terror. If not for his sake, then for Doris. Bobby shined the flashlight around, trying to get his bearings. None of it made sense. Nothing looked familiar. The collapse had transformed the entire landscape in an instant.

They were both pinned beneath what had once been the staircase. He was afraid that Doris was slipping into shock. He tried his best to keep her awake and talking. Doris complained about being cold and getting sleepy. Bobby, with some effort, removed his jacket and draped it over her. Bobby asked her about her grandchildren, her rose garden. Anything and everything he could think of. Ten long hours and about a million "our fathers" later, they were both rescued. A redheaded firefighter named Patrick O'Brien from Brooklyn stuck his head through a hole in the rubble. To Bobby, he was more beautiful than any angel depicted in the stained-glass windows of his church. Two things would never happen again after that day. He never again spoke badly about firefighters, and he never would walk without a pronounced limp or cane.

Bobby was from one of those typical large Italian families. He was the fourth of six children. Bobby had two older brothers, an older sister, and two younger sisters. The recovery was a long one, but his friends and family bombarded him with support daily. A few times, he wished he were an only child. The benefit, however, far outweighed the occasional irritation. The authorities at One Police Plaza later clarified his status. While they valued his actions and service, his time in the field was over. No one wants to see a gimpy detective. They gave him the option of riding a desk in the warrants squad or disability retirement at 75% of his salary. Bobby had little choice and picked the latter. He retired as a detective second grade, with the appreciation of a grateful city.

He suddenly jolted back to reality. "You want something to eat, Bobby?" Aunt Angie asked him. It was her diner that he always used to meet new clients.

"No, thank you, ang. Maybe after my meeting.

"What kind of client?" she asked. "One of those missing spouse cases? Or better yet, a cheater!" The seedy side of human behavior absolutely fascinated his aunt. The more indelicate, the better. She loved those unsolved murders and missing person mysteries on Dateline.

Private detective work is far from exciting, despite media depictions. Often, you are following people or staking out various locations, photographing a cheating spouse or someone who is faking an injury in an insurance claim. He was thankful for the work he could do, given his limited mobility, but he missed being with the NYPD.

"Not really sure," "The gentleman was very secretive on the phone."

"Really?" Angie said in a near fever pitch. He glimpsed his reflection in the window.

Yikes, he thought. I got to hit the gym. He was guessing his weight must be around two hundred and fifty pounds. Bobby never got on a scale except at the Doctor's office. He promised himself for the thousandth time; I am getting in shape. Treadmill, weights, and no more pasta.

Sure, like his mother would ever allow that. A gentleman walked into the diner. "Mr. Bocchini?"

"Yes," said Bobby. "You must be Mr. Adams."

"Please call me Walter." From his Brooks Brothers suit, Italian dress shoes, and matching Gucci tie, Bobby guessed he was a finance guy. It was quite a contrast to Bobby's ensemble, all of which came from the JC Penney big and tall department clearance rack.

"Can we sit here?" he said, pointing to the booth.

"Would you like some coffee?"

"Yes, please."

Angie had been waiting patiently and nearly knocked over Tina, hustling over to take their order. "Good morning, gentlemen. What would you like?" she asked, eyeing Walter curiously. Walter politely requested a black coffee. "Sure thing, sweetie."

Everyone was "Sweetie" or "Hun" to his aunt.

"Another coffee for me too," said Bobby.

"Huh, oh, sure thing." She had entirely forgotten he was there.

He got down to business after she departed. "How can I help you, Mr. Adams? You were rather vague on the phone."

"Yes, Mr. Bocchini—" "Bobby," he interrupted. "Thank you, Bobby. It's my wife, you see."

Just then, Angie returned. "Here we go, gents. Do you need anything else?"

"No, thank you," Walter said. Angie lingered, desperately trying to glean any scrap of info.

"Thank you, Angie," Bobby shooed his aunt away with a glance. He turned back to Walter. "Your wife?" Bobby inquired.

Walter nodded. "First, let me say my friend Bruce Stanley has highly recommended you."

About eight months earlier, Bruce hired Bobby when his much younger wife started spending too much time at the gym. She was, in fact, spending time with a man named Jim.

Bruce confronted her with a series of pictures Bobby provided and their marriage came to a swift and cost-effective conclusion.

"How is Mr. Stanley?" he asked.

"He is well," Walter said. "He sends his warmest regards. Let me begin by saying that I adore my wife but, to be honest, she has a problem. An affliction, really." He stared down uncomfortably at his coffee.

Bobby said nothing; in situations like this, filling the void of silence with unnecessary words makes things even more uncomfortable.

"She has suffered in the past from hypersexuality or Sexual Compulsivity. She used to be powerfully and undeniably attracted to the more salacious side of sex."

"Salacious?"

"Yes." He shifted uneasily in his seat. "Inappropriate, lewd." He was close to crying.

Angie was inching over. Bobby shot her a look that stopped her in her tracks. She unhappily retreated to the counter. His mind was racing. What exactly did he mean by that? He wondered.

"Go on if you can, Mr. Adams."

"A family member had abused her after her parents died in a car accident. Despite being under treatment for years, I am worried she is backsliding."

"How so?" Bobby asked, dreading Walter's next statement.

"It is just a feeling, really. I have no concrete evidence, mind you. She has been distant lately, defensive, you know. She has been evasive about her plans and whereabouts," he said, steadying himself with a sip of coffee.

"Any infidelity?"

"No," Walter answered. "Not since we have been married. But I am certain she is hiding something from me. We have never had secrets before. It is the cornerstone of our marriage. I need to be sure," he said, his eyes filling with tears of dread. "Can you help me?" He was almost whispering now.

"Yes, Walter," Bobby smiled compassionately. "I will absolutely help you."

"Wonderful," Walter said. "And thank you, you have been very professional as advertised."

"Thank you," Bobby said. "I can begin as soon as tomorrow. Could you provide her work and home address?"

Walter produced a large white envelope. Inside was a current picture of his wife and an incredibly detailed itinerary of her normal movements. Along with his business card. Walter, Adams, CEO, Adams, Winslow, and Chase – a very high-end capital management and arbitrage firm in Midtown Manhattan. Nailed it, Bobby thought.

"I took the liberty of putting this together," Walter said. "Mr. Bocchini, discretion is of the utmost importance in this matter."

"You have my word, Mr. Adams."

"Walter," he corrected.

"Walter," Bobby replied. "We can discuss my fee later if you are comfortable with that."

Again, Walter produced an envelope, this time with the unmistakable weight of cash. "I hope this will be a sufficient retainer," he said.

"I'm sure it will," Bobby assured him, sliding the envelope into his breast pocket. They stood and shook hands. Walter attempted to pay the bill, but Bobby shook his head. "I've got this, Mr. Adams."

Walter nodded, then turned and left; a town car pulled up in the queue and whisked him away. Inside the envelope, Bobby was stunned to find one hundred and fifty bills amounting to $15,000. "Yikes, no Uber driving this month," he said to himself. Bobby's cousin Nico came over to clear the table, followed closely by his Aunt Angie. Her eyes were wild with questions.

"So?" she asked. Smiling, Bobby said.

"So, even rich people have problems."

TWO:

DIGGING IN

Bobby maintained a small office in an old strip mall on the west side. Spartan did not fully describe it. The drab space included two desks, one for him and one that had been occupied by his now ex-wife. She was his secretary and partner when he started the private investigation agency. She feared from the beginning it was not a gold mine. Early in the relationship, her parents had cast doubts about Bobby's prospects. Her father's career as an airline pilot provided her with a privileged upbringing. Bobby and his entire family were blue collar. He was unsure of the exact moment or reason she bailed out on the relationship. It could have been his change physically, or his moody behavior after 9/11. Whatever the reason, in September 2012, her attorney served him with the divorce papers. He attempted to talk with her, but she was unmoved by his arguments, so he signed the papers and began the next chapter of his life. Women remained an intriguing mystery to most men, and he was no exception.

Bobby looked at the information on Nina Adams. From her picture, he could see she was attractive, extremely attractive. Long, brown hair, thin, fit, and just a little posh. Not the usual image of a nymphomaniac, not that he knew what that would look like. From her itinerary and LinkedIn page, she was highly active among various charities in New York. She sat on the boards of the Met, Boys and Girls clubs, and The Never Forget Foundation. The charity created scholarships for the Twin Towers victims' children. This just made little sense. How could someone of her caliber be interested in something so... What was that word? Salacious? She had grown up in Pittsburgh, Pennsylvania. Gone to Vassar, for God's sake. What he needed was to find out more about this disorder, so he called his friend Rich Gensler.

Rich oversaw NYU's Psychology department. He had volunteered his services to any police officers or firefighters affected by 9/11. Over time, Rich helped him come to terms with post-traumatic flashbacks. They had dealt with the divorce, and his unfortunate loyalty to the New York Jets. He called and asked Rich when he could work him in.

"What is happening, Bobby? Do you need to talk right now?" He was always extremely attentive.

"No, Rich, I am fine. It is a case in which I am working. I need you to help me understand something."

"Gotcha. How about tomorrow around lunchtime?" Rich asked.

"Perfect."

He considered Aunt Angie's, but dismissed it because of her tendencies to eavesdrop.

"How about that little deli near your office? My treat..."

"Wait, what? Are you sure you are, okay?"

Rich fancied himself as a comedian.

"I am fine, smart guy. See you tomorrow."

Life is funny. Two months had passed without a single case. As a result, Bobby had only been driving for Uber. In fact, his electric blue Hyundai

Elantra had made so many trips to JFK and LaGuardia that the "professional" cabbies barely flipped him off anymore. Cabbies hate Uber drivers.

Things were getting tight financially. He was thirty days behind on his mortgage but current on his car payment, but he had canceled his Hulu and Netflix accounts and anything else unnecessary. So, the retainer money was a very welcome infusion of cash.

Bobby's old C.O., Sal Mancuso, called as he was about to leave for lunch. Sal said he had something he wanted Bobby's help with. Bobby tried his best to decline, but when Sal said, "kid, just get your ass down here," he grabbed a hamburger on his way to Manhattan South. As he sat in the McDonald's drive-thru line, he looked at the image of Ronald in the kids' playland. t "Whose idea was it to use a creepy clown as a mascot? Weird. "

THREE:

A SECOND CASE

He arrived at the Police station around 1:00 pm. He wanted to pick up Nina Adams' trail as she left the board meeting at 2:30. Although Bobby had worked at the precinct for years, they made him wait, show his driver's license, and announce him before letting him see Sal. When they buzzed him in, Bobby slowly limped up the stairs. As soon as he made it to the top, he was a little out of breath, and his leg throbbed. He heard a familiar voice.

"Look, it's Bobby Bocchini, the Big Linguine!"

Bobby had known Edward Getz since his first day at the academy. They underwent training, worked in the same precinct, and took the Sergeant exam together. He did not recall doing or saying anything unkind to Ed, but the man despised Bobby for an unknown reason. He constantly made demeaning comments.

"Hi, Ed; how are you doing?" he asked, trying to be civil. "Holy crap, you are about four hundred pounds now? Put down the fork!" He laughed.

Ed was a skinny, sallow chain smoker; he smelled like a pool hall and looked a good ten years older than he was.

"Yeah, Ed, I have a little work to do," he said, biting his tongue.

"A little? You look like Shamu in a cheap suit," Getz said.

Finally, Sal showed up. "Getz, get back to work and shut your mouth. You are a week behind on your dd3s. Before your shift is over, I want them all finished."

"Wow, easy captain, I have feelings too, you know!" Ed said. He glared at Bobby one last time, and he was gone.

"Sorry, Bobby, he's an idiot!" Sal said, shaking his head. "Hey, you are moving a little better, Bobby."

"You think so?" Sal smiled.

"Definitely. Come on into my office. I have something for you."

Sal opened his door and motioned him to a chair. "Do you remember the Jessica Grant case from circa 2014?" Sal asked.

"Yeah, a young girl going to her father's office from ballet class, I think. Never made it there. No trace, as I recall."

Sal smiled at him. "Exactly. You always have had a wonderful memory." Sal sighed. "Her Dad is Thomas Grant, used to be a hotshot hedge fund manager or something."

"Used to be?" Bobby asked.

"The man cannot seem to move on. He has gone through all his money and gone out of business. His wife left him. He just will not accept that Jessica is gone. Bobby, look, I made him a promise that we would never stop until we found her."

"But," Bobby started. "Isn't the case closed?"

Sal continued. "It's more like a cold case. The bigwigs have forbidden me to spend even another dime on it." Sal rubbed his forehead. "Sal, no one, not even Mr. Grant, can say you didn't give it all you had."

One thing about Sal, his heart was always in the right place. When he promised Thomas Grant, he would find her, it was a solemn oath.

"Bobby, I want you to review the case," Sal said, almost pleading.

"Sal, the whole New York City Police Department was on this and produced nothing."

"I cannot tell that man it is over, Bobby. He is so sure, so committed."

Bobby massaged his temples, feeling a headache coming on. "Sal, if you want me to look. I will," he said. "I can't promise you or him anything, but I'll give it a shot."

He desperately wanted to say "No!" but he owed Sal a lot. Bobby wondered about having sufficient bandwidth or mobility for two cases. He had doubts about solving it at all, even with the NYPDs near infinite resources, let alone operating on his own in his current capacity and limitations.

"Excellent! Sal said. I knew I could count on you. Listen, he has nothing left." Sal gave him another envelope, the third one of the day.

"What's this?" Bobby asked.

"Per diem money."

"Look, Sal, as fate would have it—" he began.

"No arguments, kid; just do me a solid here and take it. Do your best for the poor father and that little girl." Sal paused for a second, visibly affected. His gaze shifted to the corkboard behind his desk, where a flier about Jessica remained.

"They will get the best I've got, Sal; Bobby promised. That is all I can ask, kid. Thank you!" As Bobby left the office, Ed Getz was about to speak, but Sal's angry stare made him look away.

"I'll send you copies of all the files we have," Sal said. His entire demeanor had lightened. Bobby waved as he descended the stairs. "Nice job, Bocchini!" Bobby chided himself. Sure, let us tilt at a few more windmills.

FOUR:

ON THE EDGE

Thomas Grant was at a tipping point. He was sitting in his run-down effi-
ciency apartment on the lower east side, a glass of scotch in his hand, a
9mm pistol sitting on the end table beside him. He was just so exhausted, a
fatigue you just cannot seem to sleep off. Not that he really slept, anyway. No,
truth be told, he had not slept all that well in almost seven years now. Not
since that terrible day. He remembered it like it was yesterday.

He was sitting in his office, looking at his computer screens. One
showed the company ticker symbols and daily activity on the New York Stock
exchange. Some in the green, some in the red. Most of Thomas' were green,
as usual. On the other screen, he was constantly scanning for news and ana-
lysts' estimates. It was almost time for Q3 earnings to be reported. After the
financial crisis of 2008, many people were nervous about investing, but not
Thomas. It was all like a second language to him. He had nerves of steel and
an innate sixth sense for picking winners and avoiding losers. His wealthy
clients often saw double digit returns that surpassed all the other hedge funds
in Manhattan. One or two more years and he could take the company public
or cash out. He thought about his father, a small-town accountant, and his

mother, a math teacher at the local high school. Both were brilliant, but they had played things so safely. Settling for mundane, insignificant lives in the small town of Bennington, Vermont. He already made ten times what his father had. He could send Jessica to Harvard or Princeton or pretty much any other school on the planet. Yes, he had the world by the ass.

He was watching Bloomberg Television for Alibaba's IPO announcement. He hadn't taken advantage of Amazon in the beginning, and he wasn't about to miss the train this time. His assistant Peggy popped her head in to say his wife was on line one.

"Hello" he said.

"Why is Jessica ignoring my calls?" his wife snapped.

"I do not know. Isn't she with you?" Thomas asked, only half listening to her. There was a pause.

"That's not funny Tom. Are you saying she isn't there?" He sat upright as an icy shiver went down his back.

"I thought you were dropping her here."

"No, she told me she would call you to pick her up! I was stuck in a meeting.

"Why in the hell didn't you call me directly?" Suddenly, Thomas didn't care about IPOs, Alibaba, or anything else. "Hang on!" He put her on hold and dialed the Ballet studio.

"Arabesque of Greenwich, Autumn speaking."

"Autumn, it's Thomas Grant, is Jessica still there?" he asked, barely concealing his growing panic.

"No Mr. Grant, she left about an hour ago. She said you were picking her up outside. Are you saying you didn't get her?" Now Autumn, too, was also in full panic mode.

"I'm sure she is fine," he said, trying to reassure himself as much as her. "She will probably turn up here in a moment or two. I will phone you back when she gets here."

When his wife arrived, they had an animated argument, complete with finger pointing and raised voices. Most of his employees took this as their cue to clock out for the day. They both finally realized the only important thing was finding their daughter. They called 911 and reported Jessica missing. In New York, people don't have to wait 24 hours to report missing children, older adults, and people with certain conditions. Within twenty minutes, a police officer was taking statements from both parents and getting a rundown on the timeline and a description of the girl. The officer asked for a current picture of Jessica and Thomas, picked up the sterling frame from the credenza behind him, and slipped the picture out.

"This is from two months ago."

The officer was gathering all the information when Sal walked in. The officer snapped to attention.

"At ease, officer. Mr. and Mrs. Grant, my name is Sal Mancuso, and I am the precinct captain."

It was unusual for a police C.O. to interject himself into an early stage missing person investigation, but if a child was involved. Sal made an exception. As the weeks stretched into months, Thomas spent more time trying to find Jessica, and in doing so, his business suffered. His wife Margaret withdrew from him further and further. He and Margaret went on local and national news shows asking for info about their missing daughter. On the one-year anniversary of Jessica's disappearance, Margaret had enough. She moved back in with her parents and filed for divorce shortly thereafter. Thomas was no longer the man she had fallen in love with and married. His once thriving business was failing.

He spent all day, every day, putting up flyers, going door-to-door and appearing on talk shows and podcasts. Anything to keep Jessica in the public consciousness. Eventually, Margaret met another man at a support group for parents that lost children to illness or tragedy. Thomas had no such time for support groups, therapy, or anything else that couldn't bring Jessica back home. They liquidated everything in the divorce settlement, including the house, the cars, and their investments. Thomas even sold his firm for pennies on the dollar, just to keep funding the search for Jessica. He appeared on America's Most Wanted, and a podcast called Carpe Noctem that boasted the largest national following in the True Crime genre. Each time, tips would come in, but none that lead to anything. Thomas met with Sal on a weekly basis, and he did his best to keep Thomas apprised of the case. Even the FBI could not turn up anything new.

Thomas spent at least two hundred thousand dollars on the best private investigators money could buy. They too struck out. It was as though she had just vanished. So, it went on for seven excruciating years. Thomas tried to meet other people. He even went out on a few dates, but all he could talk about was finding Jessica. There were no second dates, and that suited him just fine. When he could sleep, he would wake up only to feel that pain, and that sense of loss, waiting for him. All of which brought him to this place in time. Exhausted, both physically and emotionally. All his money was gone. He was unsure how he was going to pay for his rent, or even his next meal. He eyed the gun on the table beside him. Never had he even considered suicide before.

What if they found Jessica? He couldn't leave her all alone. But she wasn't coming back, was she? He picked up the gun and clicked off the safety.

"Forgive me Jessica. I have failed you." He closed his eyes and leaned back in his chair and took a deep breath. At that moment, the phone rang. He tried to ignore it and get to the business at hand. It rang again, and a text notification buzzed. It was from Sal. He sighed, set the gun back down and hit the redial button.

FIVE:

FOLLOW THAT TESLA

Bobby began the surveillance of Nina after her board meeting. She got into her Tesla Model S just after three pm. Nina was quite the looker, wearing a stylist Navy linen suit highlighting the ensemble; it even matched the color of her Tesla. She was trim, yet slightly curvy. He understood why Walter wanted to keep her around. She made two stops before she headed home, the first at Elizabeth Arden. The second was at Green Nation, a health food joint on Lexington Avenue. Bobby Googled it on his phone. They sold high nutrition kombucha, whatever that was, and green drinks. Now he had tried a million weight loss schemes in the past few years. Two of which he could barely swallow, let alone drink daily. Most gave him varying levels of gastric discomfort, from mild to violent. Bobby hated them all, but Nina was knocking hers back like a champion. Perhaps it was different; then he looked at the price. "Nope, not on my budget."

Nina got back in her car and drove straight home. Walter arrived home 45 minutes later. Bobby stayed for another hour and headed home at around nine pm. He would have to stock up on provisions for the job tomorrow. When on a stakeout, food was always an important consideration. One had to consume food and drink wisely because of limited restroom access. His mother had provided meals for his first few cases. On his first occasion, he had to break surveillance to allow nature to call, which resulted in him losing track of his target. The second time, the sheer mass of the meal put him to sleep. The outcome also included the loss of the target. Bobby vowed to be more professional.

These days he kept it simple: water, a few protein bars, and a little thermos of coffee. Normally, he borrowed vehicles from his siblings. The same car's presence would eventually catch anyone's attention. This time was different. He had operating funds, thanks to Walter. He arranged with the local Enterprise office to switch out cars every few days for the next week. Today it was a gray Ford Taurus. He liked this car; it had nice electronics; it was roomy—important for a stocky guy, and it blended in with the other 10,000 gray Fords around the city. He stopped by an all-night deli on his way home. Bobby always wrestled with his weight. Bobby knew he wasn't supposed to eat after 8 pm, but he was starving. He tried to rationalize the late-night snacking. He was really concerned that being heavy would make him unattractive to women. Who wants to be alone forever?

As he waited for his food, he did a web search for the missing girl. Jessica Elizabeth Grant. It pulled up pictures of her and had a synopsis of the basic facts. No history of family disturbances. There were no obvious issues with either her parents or someone wishing to do them harm. They never found a body. In fact, no trace of her since that day. Ransom was neither requested nor paid. NYPD, the FBI, and three high-priced PIs could not produce even a scrap of additional evidence. She simply vanished. Again, that gnawing doubt crept in.

"Why did I take this case? I have no chance of finding this poor little girl." There was another story on the fifth anniversary of her disappearance. It mentioned the toll it had taken on her parents. After the divorce, the mother remarried and moved out of the state. The father had bankrupted his company and spent his last dime trying to find her. Anyone would think twice about taking on a case like this. It was not like some under-funded backwater police department conducted the former investigations. This was the NYPD and the FBI; if Scotland Yard had been involved, you would have a trifecta of the three best law enforcement agencies on the planet. Yet they had struck out.

There was just something about the way Sal looked when he asked him to take the case. That and the father's unwavering determination and devotion. It went a long way with Bobby; that is a person you give 100% effort to. His panini was gone, as if by magic, and his eyelids were getting heavy, so he headed home.

As he got in the car, the envelope Sal had given him fell out of his jacket. Bobby had never looked inside. He opened the envelope and found another $3,000 inside. Earning $18k in a day or even month was a first for him. If my ex could see me now, he thought. He arrived home to the unwanted smell of weed. His neighbor Phil loved cannabis. Claiming it helped with his glaucoma, the man would say with a wink and a knowing head nod. Phil even went so far as to suggest it could help with the residual pain Bobby had. He politely declined. He was exhausted. As soon as his head hit the pillow, he fell into a deep sleep.

SIX:
WHERE DID SHE GO

The vehicle to Bobby's right suddenly exploded in a massive fireball. He could feel the heat on the side of his face. Bobby felt the blast reverberating in his chest. He tried to scramble to his feet, but ran into a... wall? Dazed, it took a few seconds for him to realize it was all just a nightmare. Before going to bed, he had Alexa set an alarm for 5:30 am. The thunderclap beat her to the punch at 4:45. Abrupt sounds like thunder or even fireworks occasionally set off his PTSD, as it had this time. He was sweating profusely; it took him ten minutes for his breathing and heart rate to return to normal. He occasionally had nightmares about falling or being buried again beneath the World Trade Center. He also had experienced traumatic events in the war.

His LAV-25 fighting vehicle was struck by an RPG in the desert near Kuwait. He lost a buddy named Tyler Bostic in the same attack. Tyler's vehicle had encountered an improvised explosive device, or IED. While Bobby's episodes were fewer and farther between now, it was not an ideal way to start the day when he felt normal. He showered and had a quick bite. For breakfast, he had one cup of coffee and a bowl of oatmeal. By 6:30, Bobby parked a block from Walter and Nina's house. It was an impressive brownstone on the Upper East Side. He tried to imagine how much that would set him back. He peeked at a real estate site and saw a comp, two blocks over, that had gone for a jaw-dropping eleven million dollars.

Bobby remembered feeling a little guilty when he saw how much cash Walter had given him the other day. The fifteen grand retainers no longer bothered Bobby in the least. He referred to Nina's schedule. She would be off to a Pilates class within the next thirty minutes. His stomach growled.

"I fed you; now shut up!" An older Asian lady was walking by and gave him a strange look. She had one of those little rat dogs rich people seem to adore. He did not like little dogs, they were too yappy. He just thought dogs should be companions with additional utility. Alerting the owner to trouble is a minimum requirement for a dog. He supposed a little dog could do that too.

Nina came out of the house. Today, Bobby had recently driven a Toyota Camry, black with gray pleather seats. He had to admit he liked the Ford a little better. Nina had on her workout clothes today. Comfortable look-ing but still expensive, she also had on one of those Apple watches and a pendant. He always paid attention to jewelry. While clothes may change for stealth, accessories typically remain the same. She pulled the Tesla out into traffic and headed west. One-person surveillance was an extremely difficult proposition. Bobby tried to put a car or two between the target and himself. He switched position, sometimes behind and sometimes off to the right. The left lane can lead to the loss of the tail. Nina pulled into a Starbucks parking lot and got out. No green drink this morning. Bobby couldn't tell what she ordered, but it was large. No, Venti, he corrected himself. She jumped back in the car and took off. This time, she really put her foot into it. He briefly fell behind, but the traffic intensified, allowing him to re-acquire the Tesla. She pulled into the gym parking lot at 8:15. According to her schedule, she was normally here for at least an hour.

Once she was inside, he looked at the abbreviated file Sal had given him at the station.

Sal promised to get him the full shebang by Saturday. That worked because Walter told Bobby that he and Nina were heading to Cape May in Jersey on Saturday and Sunday. They would be together the whole time. There was no need for him to follow. He could use the time to really dig deep into the other case.

Sal's file included a timeline, girl's photos, and a psychological evaluation of parents. Both were well-adjusted, no obvious psychosis or other red flags. No reason for either parent to profit from the little girl's disappearance. No large insurance settlements. In fact, it seemed like a paltry sum. How could someone just vanish? If she disappeared today, tracking would be so much easier. There were just so many more surveillance devices today. Smartphones, traffic cameras, security footage. The report mentioned a liquor store on the corner by the dance studio, but a UPS truck obstructed the camera's view at the time the class let out. Another nearby check-cashing place was offline for maintenance. ATMs, he thought, but they must have checked them. It could still be worth a follow up.

"Where did you go, Jessica?" he said aloud.

"Planning to sit there all day, big boy?" a voice asked from the left. "Some of us have work to do here." The man looked to be the stockbroker type. Hugo Boss suit, those pretentious little driving moccasins, and tons of attitude to go with that Boston accent. Bobby looked at his watch. There were still forty-five minutes before Nina should be done. He tried to ignore the fussy little man. He knocked on the window this time.

"Hey, asshole, I'm talking to you." Bobby sighed and stepped out of the car. The man was wearing way too much cologne. Bobby pulled himself to his full height, towering over him. The man took a step back.

"You going to move soon?" The man quickly became somewhat more civil. He began gripping the umbrella a little more like a club, tightening his grip slightly. Before the little man had any dumb ideas, Bobby unzipped his jacket, allowing it to fall open. Most days, Bobby carried a sidearm, and today was no exception. He had four pistols, but he was far from a gun nut. His were purely vocational. Today he had his forty-five-caliber browning high-power in a pancake holster. Bobby liked his Browning. It was a big pistol. Some complained it was a little too bulky. Not for Bobby, who inherited his dad's large hands. The guy caught sight of the gun and made one of those "uh oh" faces. Bobby looked him squarely in the eye and said, "No, sir, I am sorry. I will not be ready to leave for another hour. I appreciate your understanding."

The little man stammered a bit as he backed away. "Yeah, no problem. Have a wonderful day." Nice and subtle, Bobby thought. He hoped that no one had taken notice of the brief altercation, especially Nina.

SEVEN:

GIVEN THE SLIP

Nina emerged from the building on schedule. She jumped in her car and headed north to 5th Avenue. Three blocks later, she parked at the spa after making a left. According to the schedule, she always got her eyebrows waxed and massage therapy on Thursdays, and the session lasted for two hours. Bobby had enough time for the lunch meeting before she finished. He waited five extra minutes to make sure she did not double back, then he headed to Levine's Deli. He parked across the street and crossed at the light. The leg was bothering him today, more than normal. It must be about to rain again. Bobby just made it to the other curb when the light changed. A yellow cab zoomed past him, so close that he felt the street spray from the wheels.

"Jerk," Bobby yelled. "Go back to Jersey, you moron!"

As he got to the front door, Rich Gensler was standing there with a big smile on his face.

"Ah, making friends and influencing people again, I see, Bobby."

"No, Rich, if you must know, I am taking your advice and emoting, as opposed to keeping bottled up inside." Rich chuckled. "Eureka! Progress at last!" "Come on, you big lug, let's grab lunch."

"Why, Doctor Gensler, I believe you were body shaming me," Bobby said jokingly. "Now Bobby, you know Big Lug is a term of affection."

They both laughed and walked up to the counter. The owner, Rich's friend, signaled them to the end.

"Abe," Rich said. "How is the corned beef today?"

"Doc, if it were any finer, it would be a controlled substance," Abe replied. They all laughed.

"In that case," Rich said, "I'll take the Rubin combo, please."

"What would you like, young man? Abe asked jovially.

"I'll take the Abe Special." That comprised hot corned beef, pastrami, Swiss cheese, and Russian dressing.

"His diet started tomorrow!" he assured himself.

"You want fries with that?" Abe asked.

"No sir, just the sandwich and an iced tea, please."

"Go grab a seat, coming right up."

They arrived after the lunch rush and sat at a back table.

Embarrassed about the topic to be discussed, Bobby reluctantly took a deep breath.

"So Rich, Hypersexuality, what the hell is that all about?"

"Bobby, is there anything you want to tell me first? Your feelings are nothing to be ashamed of, as I always say. It is a shame if you cannot admit your own weaknesses."

"We all, and I mean all of us, have things we would like to hide away, but that doesn't mean you should."

It was just like Rich. You could tell him the deepest fear or kink, and he would just smile and say, "Ok, let's delve into that a little further."

"No, Rich, honestly, I am working on a case for a prominent local financier, and he is afraid his wife has sexual compulsivity."

Abe walked up with their lunch. If he had heard anything, he did not say a word or show any odd reactions. Being a restaurant owner in a diverse city, he had heard everything. They dug into their sandwiches for a few moments; Bobby loved delis; the smells alone were worth the trip.

Rich filled him in. "I am not an expert on the topic. It is mainly men who have it, although 20% of the people struggling with it are women. It normally begins in childhood, some traumatic event, or, perhaps, abuse. Later in life, it can manifest itself sexually."

"Can they cure it?" Bobby asked.

"Cured?" Rich shifted a little. "More like controlled. It just depends on the person," Rich said.

"The husband mentioned evidence of a potential relapse in her treatment."

Rich quipped. "Sorry. I couldn't resist. If there's infidelity, it is worrying. I am told there can be a seedy side to it all: sex clubs, anonymous partners. That certainly is an obstacle. Do you know anyone with the condition?" he asked.

"I am following her, and she hasn't strayed from her normal schedule, but who knows?"

"Do we truly recognize that this is an issue, or is the husband simply guessing?"

"He's paying me a hefty sum," Bobby said.

"Gotcha," Rich replied. "Give me a few days, and I'll check around for you, okay?"

They finished their lunch. Bobby proudly paid the bill, and they left. Rich promised to get back to him in a day or two.

"Bobby, you're walking better, aren't you?"

He had not noticed, but Rich was the second person to say so in two days.

"So, I guess it could be."

Bobby returned to his car and headed uptown to pick up the tail. He arrived just as Nina was walking out. Everything was right on schedule. As she walked up to the car, she pulled out her phone, punched a couple of keys, and then hailed a cab.

Shit, Bobby thought. He got behind the Taxi and followed it just as traffic became heavy. At Lexington and 101st, Nina got out, paid the fare, and hopped into a cab going the opposite way.

"What the?" he sputtered. She either noticed someone was following her, or she was being extraordinarily careful. Impossible for him to know which one.

Regardless, he was hopelessly stuck in traffic, headed in the wrong direction. Nina was soon out of his sight and gone to God only knows where, to meet up with God only knows who. He took the only option available. Bobby doubled back, hoping to park near her car. Eventually, she would have to return for it. At least, he hoped so. Damn it, Bobby thought, I really need this job.

Do I really have to tell Walter? Bobby's moral compass immediately overrode the thought. Of course, you do. Shit!

EIGHT:

I DON'T LIKE WHERE THIS IS HEADED

It took him twenty minutes to get back to Nina's car. The Tesla was right where she left it. That was naturally both good and bad, a mixed situation; she had to come back, but Bobby was still unaware of her whereabouts. Forty-five minutes later, a blue Honda Accord pulled up to her car. It carried the same Uber sign he had in his Hyundai. She got out and jumped into her car. She started it up, pushed the button, or did whatever you do to start a Tesla. Perhaps an incantation invoking the name of Elon Musk. That made him chuckle. She backed up and pulled out into traffic. The Uber driver pulled out, too. He wondered where he picked her up from. They traveled in the same direction for about ten blocks. Nina appeared to be heading home, signaling to turn right at the stoplight, but who knew after tonight? Time to decide. He could verify she went home, or follow the driver. He settled on the latter, being almost certain that Nina was on her way home. The driver got out of the car and stepped inside a Seven Eleven. Bobby parked, got out of his vehicle, and started following him in. Then an alternative plan came to him.

Sal had given Bobby credentials to work on the Jessica Grant case. It said NYPD consultant, but it did not have a shield on it. Bobby had his gold shield, but it clearly had retired on the top rocker. The poor lighting could mask the difference if he flashed the badge quickly. The driver emerged and got in his car. Bobby approached and tapped the driver's side window.

"Good evening, sir," he said as officially as he could. "License and registration. Bobby was polite yet firm. The driver asked what the problem was. He flipped open the badge holder for a couple of seconds, then he snapped it shut.

"Your last fare," he said. "Where did you pick her up?" "I can't tell you that," the driver responded defensively. "You can't?" Bobby asked. "Are you aware that withholding information, in a case like this, is a class A felony?" He lied.

"Felony?" the driver stammered. "Wait, wait; I have the address right here.

"A hotel on Bowery Street? You are certain this is where you picked up your last fare?

"Yes," the driver replied. He also produced his vehicle registration and license. Bobby took both back to his car, just like an actual police officer would do. As he sat in his car pretending to call the information in, he snapped a picture of both documents and headed back.

"Here you go, sir. Thank you for your cooperation."

Ok, so he was a little ashamed of himself and a little concerned. Impersonating an officer could land him in jail, not to mention cost him his pension. He let that sobering thought sit for a minute. The driver put the car in drive, signaled correctly, and drove well under the speed limit. Bobby followed him for a few blocks to mess with him. Bobby turned right and arrived at Nina's house in ten minutes. He caught a glimpse of her passing the window. He wondered where she had gone. That was a very sneaky veteran maneuver. He thought about heading back home, but he knew himself well enough to know he could not fall asleep without knowing. So, he headed uptown.

Bowery Street in lower Manhattan was not exactly the part of town he imagined Nina would frequent. A couple of forgettable Chinese joints, a lighting outlet, and three rough-looking bars. As he crossed over East Houston, Bobby saw a fleabag hotel. He held his breath for a second. Private investigators are expected to be unbiased and report facts only. He was hoping Walter was wrong about his wife. He seemed like a nice guy, and Nina was gorgeous and sophisticated.

As he pulled in front, he realized his worst suspicions. The Palace, the sign announced proudly. Yikes! He thought. This joint looks like it would have hot and cold running bedbugs.

He dragged himself out of the car, his leg swollen and aching from sitting too long in the car. He limped across the street and entered The Palace. The upholstered chairs in the front lobby had several terrible-looking stains. Also, a brown pleather recliner with a sign that said, "reserved for the King!" All the chairs sat in a semicircle around an ancient TV. It looked like one his parents had back in the seventies. Naturally, they had WWE wrestling on, and it totally engrossed the whole "Hee-Haw" gang. The counter was empty, and he eyed the rusty bell on the desk, questioning his last tetanus shot before ringing it. Nothing. Bobby rang it a second time, again nothing. He was about to launch it across the room, but the Concierge arrived. He looked exactly like Uncle Fester from the Addams Family.

"Keep your damn shirt on, fat boy. I was in the shitter!"

Charming, Bobby thought. There is an image that will stay with you for a while.

"Sorry," he said to Fester. "I am wondering if you have seen this lady here tonight?" He produced a picture of Nina. He looked and smiled.

"Who wants to know?"

With some trepidation, he pulled out his semi-valid badge and flashed it at him.

"That don't mean nothing to me, cop." Fester grinned, his teeth a grisly greenish, brownish tint.

"Well then, perhaps I can appeal to your civic duty. Maybe my friend can convince you." Bobby pulled out a hundred, thinking it was a twenty. Fester's eyes nearly popped out of his skull.

"Well, my friend," Fester said, "why didn't you say so?"

"Please have a seat." He tried to usher him to the king's chair, but Bobby declined.

"I don't want any trouble with the Monarchy," he said.

The man twisted his face in confusion and scratched his bald head.

"What?"

"Sorry, never mind. You were saying?"

"Oh yeah, now I remember. She's a freak." He flashed that gorgeous smile again. "She was actually here earlier this evening."

"Was she here with anyone?" he asked. "That will require another visit from Mr. Franklin," Fester said, a bit nervously.

Bobby protested, but then he remembered his large retainer from Walter. He opened his wallet, took out a bill. Fester looked intently at the C-Note.

"Information first," he said.

"Ok, first these are crazy, dangerous people. So, I am not testifying to any of this."

Perfect for Bobby, since he really was no longer a cop.

"The lady arrived a month ago. She asked if I knew a man named Orik. An Ormanian,"

"Do you mean Armenian? Bobby asked.

"That's what I fucking said!" Fester said, looking indignant.

"My bad, go on."

"I told her I would consider it for the right price. If you know what I mean?" Fester winked, and Bobby nearly threw up. "Some ladies like a bald man. 'Cause of all the testosterone."

He stared blankly at Fester.

"Anyway," he continued. "She was not really into me, so we agreed on $100, just like you." He laughed again. "So, I called this guy named Nemo who runs some sort of club for freaks like her, and he works for this dude Orik. He came by and picked her up." Fester chucked.

"Any idea where they might have gone?" Bobby asked.

"No, somewhere in Brooklyn," Fester said. "Oh, he blindfolded her in the car."

His heart sank; it seemed Walter was right.

"How do I find this Nemo?" Bobby asked.

"You aren't listening, you do not find him. You call a number, and he finds you."

"Okay, let's call him."

"Nope," Fester said. "Nemo is a dangerous dude." He tried to snatch the bill from his hand, but he tightened his grip.

"No deal," Bobby said. "Look, it is dangerous, man. If you bust him. I would be a dead man walking," Fester said, and he was probably right.

"How often does this little circus come to town?"

"Twice a month," Fester said. "Next time someone buys a ticket, you call me right away."

Bobby let go of the bill. He took out another $100. Fester had a look of euphoria. He reached out for Franklin, but Bobby tore it in half. Half for you, half after my call. Bobby had seen that in a Humphrey Bogart movie long ago and always wanted to do that.

"Deal," Fester said, taking his half.

"Talk to you soon." Bobby turned and left. He desperately wanted to wash his hands. Hell, he wanted to burn his clothes and take a shower, but he drove four blocks to a CVS and bought a package of bleach wipes and hand sanitizer. He drove away, feeling a little dejected. Should he call Walter and give him an update? Tell him that his fears might be true? Bobby decided he wanted concrete proof that she was being unfaithful and possibly unsafe before he dropped that bombshell. He drove home, threw his suit in the dry-cleaning hamper, and showered. He turned on the TV after lying down, despite it being past midnight. Braveheart was on. Bobby set the timer on the TV for an hour and watched a little. His mind finally drifted into neutral, and he fell asleep.

NINE:

A LITTLE BRUNCH, A LITTLE DOUBT AND INSPIRATION

S aturday Morning! Universally loved by everyone. No school and, for many, no work. Bobby's usual routine included sleeping in, doing laundry, paying bills, and catching up on a few TV shows. The absolute best part, though, was his mom's brunch. She prepared bacon, eggs, waffles, and various Italian dishes every Saturday. Now, most Italians are fussy about their gravy — you might call it spaghetti sauce, but to real Italians, it is gravy. Bobby was far from impartial. His mom, in his estimation, made the world's best. She started with the meat, sausage, and ground sirloin. She browned it all and sauteed onions for a little extra punch. Then she worked in garlic. She got fresh garlic and cut it with a razor, paper thin. A little olive oil, a little heat in a cast iron pan, and the garlic liquified. Then the meat went in. She made him promise not to reveal the remaining ingredients in the sauce, but he can confirm that it is heavenly, ambrosia. She also made her own pasta, normally fettuccine. This Saturday would be a working lunch. Sal said he would stop by with the remaining documents from the Jessica Grant case. Upon arriving at the old homestead, Bobby noticed an unfamiliar car in the driveway. It did not belong to Sal. His work car was a white Dodge Charger, and Sal's personal car was much faster, a vintage '65 Chevy Corvette Stingray. Rally Red, with red leather seats, a 396 "big block", with 425 unruly horses. Just like his mom's cooking… a masterpiece. Instead, there was an ugly brown scion that needed a good wash and four new tires.

As he walked through the back door into the kitchen door, Bobby heard his mother laugh. "Pace yourself, Eddy; there is plenty more where that came from." As Bobby rounded the corner, he shuddered involuntarily. There was his saint of a mother sitting across from dead-eyed Ed Getz. "Eddy," as his mother called him, was sitting in front of a big bowl of pasta. What a nightmare. His two greatest enemies, Ed Getz and complex carbohydrates, were together in his family kitchen.

"Roberto!" His mom jumped up and ran over to give him a big hug and a kiss.

"Bocchini," Getz said. It was undoubtedly the nicest thing he had ever said to Bobby. "I got to be going, Mrs. B." Getz smiled a pleasant smile. He surprisingly had perfect teeth.

"My pleasure, sweetie; stop by anytime," his mom said, and she really meant it. She was just that kind of woman. As he turned to face Bobby, his smile turned into a scowl. "I have your boxes in the trunk," he said. They transferred the boxes into Bobby's car, a brand-new Honda Accord. He had stopped by the rental shop. Getz looked back at his house.

"Did she mean it when she said I could come back?" Getz asked in a childlike voice. Bobby's initial thought was "No, you asshole, she did not. But there was just something sad in his eyes, lonely. Of Course, she did," Bobby said. "Everyone is welcome at her house." He smiled. "Have a good day, Bobby." He turned and got in his filthy car and drove away. Bobby felt horrible. He never considered that "Eddy" was just a broken and lonely guy. "Nope, screw that!" He concluded. Getz was still a jackass.

He joined his mom back in the kitchen. Per usual, it was a wonderful, chaotic scene that had played out in his parents' house for years. His siblings, their kids, his parents all laughing, all kidding each other. His dad, Big Tony, was sitting at the head of the table, playing traffic cop, routing and rerouting massive plates of pasta, sauce, and various breakfast foods. The children were running around and laughing. They had a smaller picnic style table, just off to the side.

"Bobby, some charming friend you got there," his brother Gio, short for Giancarlo, said. "Where did you find him? The morgue?"

"Hey, go easy; not everyone can have the Bocchini's good looks."

Antonio laughed.

"What are you talking about?" his sister Maria said. "They adopted you." She laughed.

"Maria!" mom interjected. "All my children are beautiful, and all of them are all mine!"

"Yep, and she has the stretch marks to prove it!" his dad said. His mom reached out and gave him a playful swat across the face. "I am just kidding you, my love. You are the world's most beautiful woman!"

That got him a smile from his mother and a big kiss on the cheek.

"Amor Mio," she said.

"Now sit down and eat, please, before it's all gone," dad said.

Bobby's parents had one or those 18-carat gold relationships. They were devoted to one another in a way you don't see often. Bobby sat beside his two younger sisters, Francesca, Franny for short, and Giada. They all enjoyed forty-five minutes of consuming way too many calories and talking about Jets Football with his dad and brothers. Bobby helped clean up and got ready to leave. Bobby's mom asked about the files.

"It's a case Sal has me working on, Mom."

"Are you back with NYPD?" she asked.

"No, just consulting on a cold case."

"Oh, yeah?" Her curiosity perked up. His mom, just like her sister Angie, found Bobby's work fascinating. "Which one?" she asked.

"The Jessica Grant case from a few years ago," he said. It was pointless trying to keep anything from his mom. She had better interrogation skills than the most hardened KGB or CIA operative.

"Oh, Bobby, I remember that case," she said sadly. "That poor little girl. If anyone can find her, it is you." She took his face in her hands and kissed me on both cheeks. "I can't imagine what I would do if someone took one of my kids."

"Really?" Bobby said. "I know precisely what you would do. You would hunt them down like Wyatt Earp and take care of them," he said, and meant every word.

His Mom's family was 100% Sicilian, people not to be messed with.

"Damn straight!" his dad said. "Their remains would pop up in the east river for years to come."

His Mom laughed and handed Bobby a doggie bag because there was ALWAYS a doggie bag. Bobby placed the leftovers in the car. There was a nagging doubt in the back of his mind. Sure, he thought to himself. In a city of eight million, locating a seven-year-old ballerina should be a piece of cake. He shook his head. No, she would be fourteen now. He thought about giving the case back to Sal. Surely there must be someone else more... capable? he wondered.

Just then, his dad tapped on his window. "You okay sport?" he asked. Bobby rolled the window down.

"It's all good, dad," Bobby said half-heartedly.

"Come on, son, you can't kid a kidder."

After a moment's pause, Bobby said, "Dad, I'm afraid I may be in over my head on this case Sal gave me." He filled him in on the details. Dropping the garbage bags in the can. His dad leaned in on the passenger side window.

"Did I ever tell you about your Great Grandfather Pietro?"

Bobby thought for a second. "Not really."

"He was a day laborer, in a small town called Tolfa, near Rome. He raised eleven children by working twelve-hour days. Six days a week. I once confessed to him I was afraid that I did not possess that kind of strength. He told me, 'We build strength only in moments of perseverance.'"

By that point, Bobby's mom had joined Tony. "If it were one of you kids, or your mom lost out there and I could choose anyone past or present to search for them, I would choose you every day of the week, and twice on Sundays. Do you know why?"

Bobby shook his head. "Because you are all heart. Bobby, if she *is* still alive, you may be the last chance that little girl has left. You can do it. Find your strength, son."

Bobby slowly nodded, his resolve growing.

"Thanks Pop!" He smiled and waved to his parents as he backed out of the driveway.

"Wow, I did not know your grandfather was such a Mensch." Bobby's mom said as they watched him drive away.

Tony smiled. "He wasn't. He was the town drunk. A lazier man never walked the face of the earth."

"What?!" she bellowed.

"Hey, he needed a little fatherly inspiration. I couldn't think of any. So, I created some on the fly."

"You mean you lied!" she corrected, feigning indignation.

Tony smiled. "No, I improvised."

"What am I going to do with you?" she asked as she wrapped her arms around his neck. "Well, you could get me some more of your cannoli?"

TEN:

BE STILL MY HEART

B obby stopped by the Staples closest to his dungeon/office. He upgraded things a bit with a couple of six feet by four feet whiteboards, a nice desk lamp, and one of those long white tables you see at church bake sales. As he was walking out, he heard a woman yell, "Stop him! He grabbed my purse!"

Bobby looked up to see a skinny kid about sixteen years old streaking towards him. Bobby realized he had no chance of catching him. The beautiful thing about aging, though, is that it brings with it wisdom. As the kid got to within three feet of him, Bobby slid one of the white boards directly in front of him. The thief amazingly sidestepped the obstacle, but in doing so, he lost his balance and collided with a parking meter. He crashed to the ground, knocking all the air out of his lungs. Seeing the young man in distress, Bobby immediately rushed to assist him.

Bobby returned the woman's purse and waited for the police to arrive. After giving his statement to the officers, the woman tried to give him a reward for stopping to help her. Bobby thanked her but declined. He shook his head. It's nuts, he thought. Everyone is trying to give me money this week. When he arrived at his office.

He attached whiteboards to the wall, set up the table, and placed all the boxes in Jessica's case on the left. Bobby knew the first part of any investigation involved organizing data. Forensics, victim profiles, and any witness interviews. The FBI collected a large amount of data regarding the kidnapping. The wonderful thing about all the documents being copied was that they were all his, no need to keep everything separate. He could co-mingle as he saw fit. He noticed how thorough the NYPD and FBI were. Again, this caused him to wonder if he was doing the right thing.

His dad was right if Jessica was still alive. Then someone should search for her. He looked at the parents' file: no criminal record, no financial struggles, no large insurance policies. No obvious foes or disaffected employees from the husband's business. The little girl's ballet school owner's record was clean. Autumn Woods. The name sounded almost lyrical; he thought. She was forty years old and from the photo beautiful. There was no gang-related activity in the area, no similar cases, or discernable patterns. It surprised him that his findings yielded no results. She just disappeared. Bobby taped the photos of anyone connected to the issue on the left whiteboard. Foremost, Jessica. He drew a timeline on the board to the right. Jessica leaves her house at 7:10 am, driven by her mom, he thought. She arrives at school at 7:25 am. The security footage timestamps that. She goes through her morning classes, has lunch, then has geometry. "Odd for a seven-year-old," Bobby said aloud. Also, American History and gym classes. The bell rang at 3:00 pm; the security footage showed Jessica and her friend Amanda being picked up by Amanda's mom at 3:08 outside the front gate. Jessica's ballet class started at 3:30 pm. It lasted one hour and 15 minutes. Normally, Jessica's mom would pick the girls up, but Amanda had a dental appointment that day, so her mom picked her up early from class. Jessica's mom was stuck in a meeting, so she instructed Jessica to call her father to pick her up. She did not make the call. Neither Thomas nor her mother would have approved of her walking the five blocks alone.

The ballet studio had no security camera, nor did the Mexican place across the street. Detectives analyzed the footage from the ATM in the City

Bank foyer on the corner. No Jessica. So, she potentially headed south, but her dad's office was north and west of the studio. She should have walked right past the bank. The Blockbuster, located a couple of blocks down, was closing its doors and had no footage. He moved down the block, two vacant storefronts and no cameras. The next security footage was the 7-Eleven on the opposite corner, three blocks down. Nothing. In certain areas of the town, they mounted police box cameras on poles, usually in high-crime zones. But Greenwich was a wealthier area. No box was necessary. He decided he needed an actual view of the crime scene, if you could call it that.

Bobby pored over the data, and it surprised him that three hours had passed. His body felt stiff when he stood up. He shut off the lights, which reminded him that his electric bill was past due. He locked the door and walked across the street to his car. His aching knee and ankle confirmed that the humidity was on the rise. Rain was coming soon. He arrived at the ballet studio around 4:30, later than Jessica's expected walk time. It was slightly different because it was a Saturday. Bobby leaned against the building for five or six minutes, taking in the scenery and getting a feel for the area. Nothing seemed menacing; nothing seemed overtly out of place. He removed his iPhone, put it into panorama mode, and got a 360-degree perspective. Once again, nothing too unusual. People walking, driving, just living out their daily lives.

Where are you, Jessica, and why did you take the wrong route to your dad's office?

"May I be of help?" a polite woman asked. As Bobby turned, he saw Autumn Woods, the owner of the Ballet school. He recognized her from her file photo. She was about five feet four inches and had that willowy thin, yet powerful build of a dancer.

"Yes, Ma'am, my name is Bobby Bocchini. I mean Robert Bocchini." He handed her one of his cards. "I am a private investigator looking into the Jessica Grant disappearance."

"I see," a sad, tearful frown replaced her cheerful smile. "The school is now more famous for Jessica's disappearance than for ballet. Would you like to go inside? I was just locking up for the day, but...."

"That is unnecessary; I can come back another time if you need to get home to your family."

"No," she replied with a faint smile. "That is not a problem. No one is waiting for me."

What a shame, he thought. "Are you interested in grabbing a coffee or something?" Bobby asked. She said "sure" after an uncomfortable pause. "Why not?"

She took him to a small diner nearby. An older couple ran it. They looked to be in their mid-sixties. They saw Autumn, and they came around from behind the counter and hugged her.

"Sweetie, where have you been?" the older woman asked. "It's been months. I was afraid you had closed the studio, and they had turned your school into something completely depressing, like a Gap or an H&R Block." They laughed.

"Nope, not getting rid of me that easy," Autumn said.

"Ernie, clean off that little booth in the corner for Autumn and her friend."

"Oh my," she said, "you are a big one, aren't you?" She stepped back to get a clearer view of Bobby.

"Darla, this is Mr. Bocchini. He is looking into the Jessica Grant case," Autumn said.

Ernie had finished bussing the table and came to within six inches of Bobby. He was about the same height and about thirty pounds lighter. "You sure he isn't bothering you, Autumn? I can toss him out on his ear."

Both women laughed, but Bobby could tell Ernie was completely serious. He gave Bobby a disapproving glance, as if judging by his suitability for his daughter. Bobby remembered that look from his Ex's dad.

"Now, now, my big tough bear," Darla said, "I'm sure he will behave himself with our Autumn."

"Well, he better," Ernie said. "I'm a Marine."

Bobby wanted to tell him he, too, was a Marine. Instead, he just smiled as they walked back to the booth. They sat down, and Darla brought over two glasses of water and menus. The glasses were mason jars, which Bobby found charming.

"Sorry about that," Autumn said. "They kind of adopted me after my husband left and Jessica disappeared. Don't let Ernie get to you. Ernie is a former Marine, I think."

"There is no such thing as a former Marine," Bobby said. "Once a Marine, always a Marine," Bobby affirmed.

"That sounds like the voice of experience." Autumn smiled.

"Yes, ma'am, guilty as charged. Marine expeditionary force during the Gulf War."

"I imagine you have some stories," she said.

"Every Marine has stories," Ernie said with a grin. "Some of them are even true. Gunnery sergeant, Ernie Sorenson." He offered his hand. "Lieutenant Robert Bocchini." Bobby stood and shook his hand. "Semper Fi," he said.

"Oorah," Ernie responded. "Sorry about busting your balls earlier, Lieutenant."

"No problem, Gunny," he said. "Ever vigilant."

"Do you kids know what you want?"

"I'll take that Wedge Salad," Autumn said.

"How about you, Lieutenant?" he asked.

"Call me Bobby. All my friends and fellow Marines do. I'll have whatever the Gunny recommends."

Ernie nodded his approval and headed back to the kitchen.

As he sat down, it obviously impressed Autumn. "Wow, I have never seen him warm up to anyone like that." The late afternoon sunlight made her auburn hair take on a warm glow. The hue of her eyes resembled that of cognac. Bobby felt the blood rush to his cheeks. That made her laugh. "Are you blushing?" she asked.

"No, just a little warm," he said and removed his jacket. What the hell are you doing? He thought. You are in the middle of two cases and acting like a lovesick schoolboy!

"So Autumn, I read the file on Jessica, but what I need is more background. What type of kid was she? Was she a talented student?" Between the NYPD and the FBI, he had information a mile wide but no real depth. Autumn had a sad, faraway look on her face.

Jessica was her favorite student, she said. "She had a real zest for life. She had so many interests. Ballet, as well as old movies, chess, and mathematics. Her dream was to become a filmmaker. She told me that once in confidence. Her parents, no… just her mother, thought it was a waste of time and pushed her to be more serious about her grades and her dance."

"And her dad?" Bobby asked.

"She was unquestionably Daddy's little girl. He would indulge her, take her to museums, and encourage her to write stories, even screenplays. She even gave me one to read a few weeks before she disappeared."

"Really? What was it about?" he asked.

Autumn stared at the ground. "Frankly, Bobby, I never actually read it. My Ex and I were going through a rough time then, and it preoccupied me with my own problems." Her eyes brimmed with tears. Fortunately, Darla appeared with their food.

"Here we go, my dears," she said, placing the plates in front of them. "Is everything okay?" she asked.

"Bobby asked about Jessica, and it brought back memories," Autumn said.

"That looks wonderful." He looked down at his plate, and the gunny had given him Grilled Chicken Alfredo.

"Ernie told me to tell you it's the chef's specialty." Darla laughed. "Bon appétit!" She walked back to the kitchen. He stared at it for a second or two. Bobby was 100% Italian; both parents were born in Italy. He was skeptical about diner fettuccini, prepared by a Swedish-American marine gunnery sergeant. He looked up, and Autumn was staring at him.

"Well," she said.

"Right." He took his spoon and fork, swirled a few noodles into a tight circle, and popped it in his mouth. Unbelievably, it was good... exceptionally good! He took another bite, and again, it was delicious. He tried the chicken that sat atop the pasta. It was tender, perfectly grilled, and once again delicious. A truly terrible thought percolated in his head. It was not just as good as his mom's... it was, in fact, better. Few things are as sacred to an Italian boy as his mother's cooking. She can never find out, he thought.

"Is it alright?" Autumn asked with a devilish little grin—as though she already knew the answer. Ernie appeared.

"What do you think, Bobby?" he asked. "I was a little nervous to give a Goombah pasta, but what the heck,"

"To be honest, Ernie, it is the best Alfredo sauce I have ever had."

Now Autumn, Ernie and Darla burst into laughter.

"See, I told you it was good," Autumn said.

"Just one thing, though," he said. "You need to promise, no, guarantee, that my mother will never know! It would positively kill her."

Everyone laughed again. "No, really, I'm serious!"

ELEVEN:

JUST DON'T TELL MY MOTHER

They finished dinner, including dessert, an amazing Limoncello cake with mascarpone icing. "Ernie missed his life's calling. He is the Michelangelo of the greasy spoon universe." Autumn laughed Ernie and Darla were closing but told them there was no hurry. "Autumn, can you tell me which direction Jessica headed? I checked all available footage toward her dad's office." Autumn's brow furrowed. No, the Police, and FBI asked me the same question. I sometimes replay that day in his head. A single tear ran down her cheek. "I think if only I were not so preoccupied. Why didn't I walk her out to the car? Better yet, to her dad's office. It would have taken me ten minutes." She cradled her head in her hands. "Look," Bobby said, holding her hands. "You are not to blame for her disappearance. Autumn, I will find out what happened," he said, gazing into her eyes. She smiled and pulled his hand to her cheek. Oh boy, he thought. You are a dead man. She laughed. "Bobby, you're blushing again." Yep, dead man. Bobby paid the bill, rather he tried to pay it, but Ernie clarified no bill was forthcoming. So, he left a $30 tip under his dessert plate, and they left. He walked Autumn back to her apartment and made sure she got in safely. In one of his trademark awkward moments, he tried to shake hands with her, and again, she laughed. "You are one of a kind, Bobby Bocchini." One of a kind, he thought. Normally, people follow that with "but," and then she kissed him lightly on the cheek. She looked back, gave him a 50,000-volt smile, and closed her front door. When he heard both deadbolts slide home, he made his way back to his car. Bobby arrived at 11:00 PM. He did not even mind the parking ticket because of his buoyant mood. Walter and Nina would be back Sunday night. He would have to pick the surveillance backup on Monday. Bobby committed himself to both cases. He toyed with the idea of returning to the office, but decided he needed divine intervention. So, he did what any good Catholic would do. He headed to Midnight Mass. As Bobby arrived at St. Thomas, he heard a familiar voice behind me. "Bobby." He attempted to disregard it. "Bobby! Roberto Luca Bocchini!!" Uh oh, all three names, he thought. She was serious. "Oh, hi, Mom." She and Angie were sitting two pews behind him. Bobby received an intense mom look, and he dutifully took his place beside her. She and Angie both hugged him. "It's Father Michael this evening!" Angie said with glee. You would have thought they were waiting for Springsteen to come out on stage. His Aunt and Mother were groupies for certain priests, and by far their favorite was Father Michael. Bobby found it weird and asked his dad about it once. He simply said, "Look, as long as I don't have to take them, it could be Father Antonio Banderas, for all I care." As people settled in, his mom slung her arm around his neck and pulled him close enough to kiss his cheek again. His ex-wife always thought his mother was too affectionate. "What's that I smell?" his mom asked. Uh oh, maybe Autumn had transferred some of her perfume. "It smells like Alfredo Sauce. Oh, Bobby, tell me you haven't been to The Olive Garden again!" He still felt guilty for his love for Ernie's pasta. Fortunately, he came to the right place.

TWELVE:

AN UNCOMFORTABLE CONVERSATION

As his eyes flickered open on Sunday morning, Bobby was in a buoyant mood. Partly because the weather was perfect, sunny, not too warm. There was a scent in the air that reminded him of fall and football, yet it was more than that. He arrived home after Mass and floated off to bed. When he closed his eyes, he could only see Autumn's beautiful face. Okay, so, she is a pretty girl, but he had seen pretty girls before. Get a grip, he thought. Bobby replayed the scene at her door repeatedly. Putz, he thought. Yes, by all means, let's shake hands. After a little more self-flagellation, he drifted off to a deep sleep. Bobby headed to the kitchen and started his coffee maker. He slid out the filter cup, and the grounds from yesterday were waiting to greet him. He refilled the cup with a fresh filter and coffee and hit the brew button. Just then, his cell buzzed, and it changed both his mood and the trajectory of the day. His plan was to work for an hour or two, create a report for Walter about his wife's first week, and then go to his father's club to watch the Jets game. They had drafted a fresh-faced quarterback, who was supposed to be the second coming of Joe Namath. All of that would have to wait.

"Hello," he said.

"Mr. Bocchini?" the voice on the line asked.

"Yes,"

"My name is Thomas Grant; I am Jessica's father."

Oh, shit! He thought. This call was both expected and dreaded by Bobby. "Yes, Mr. Grant, I've been meaning to call you." Which was true, but he was hoping to have something to tell him. Other than that, I think I'm in love with your daughter's ballet teacher, he thought. Wait, could that be true?

"Mr. Bocchini?" he was saying.

"Yes, Mr. Grant, sorry, I have been going over the files, getting my bearings with the case." He was about to tell him that, unfortunately, he had uncovered absolutely nothing new.

"You know," Thomas said, "I was about to the end of his rope. I know at some point I must move on with my life, but I cannot let her go." Bobby could tell he was on the edge of losing his composure. "But I've known Sal for years, and he said you are one of the most insightful and gifted detectives he ever worked with. It has been a while, but I suddenly feel optimistic again. I was hoping to meet you for lunch," he said. Please do not say at 1pm, Bobby thought.

"Around 1:00, if possible? Unless you have other plans." Now Bobby could be an insensitive jerk, like most guys, but to delay the meeting with a desperate father just so he could watch the Jets lose?

"Sure, I can do that. Where would you like to meet?"

Thomas did not have a preference, so Bobby suggested Ernie and Darla's place. He confirmed he knew it well and would arrive at 1:00.

Bobby got to the restaurant about ten minutes early, although the booths were packed. Darla recognized him and came over to embrace him as if they were longtime acquaintances. He got the impression that Darla rarely considered anyone a stranger.

"Bobby!" she said. "Are you meeting Autumn again?" she asked with a sheepish grin.

"No, Ma'am, it is more of a business meeting. I am meeting with Thomas Grant."

"Oh," she said. "That poor, poor man. Follow me. You will need a little privacy." She cleared out the back booth of the diner.

Normally, that is where she and Ernie would sit to get off their feet for a few moments.

"Thank you," he said.

"Menus? she asked.

"Please." Bobby loved diners. They were vibrant, alive, and, in this case, smelled wonderful. Manhattan was a city of restaurants. Bobby had read somewhere that the city had at least twenty thousand. The room was full of people he imagined were locals. His feelings were confirmed when Thomas Grant walked in. A hush fell over the room. Both Darla and Ernie immediately met him at the door. They exchanged hugs, and several others approached him with similar greetings. It was very moving. New Yorkers often get a bad rap as jaded, self-absorbed assholes, but since 9/11, everyone seemed nicer, a little more connected. When Thomas made his way toward the booth, Bobby stood.

"Mr. Grant," he said, "I'm Robert Bocchini."

"Please call me Tom," he said.

"Only if you call me Bobby." They both smiled and sat down. A sharp pain shot through Bobby's knee, and he grimaced.

"Are you okay?" Thomas asked, then he noticed his cane sitting next to Bobby. "Just an old injury," he replied. They ordered; Thomas had a club sandwich, and Ernie recommended the Mushroom Risotto, so again, with more than a touch of guilt, Bobby agreed. Thomas was barely recognizable from the file photos. Bobby knew people changed over the years. Thomas had aged at an accelerated rate. He was thinner and paler, with dark circles under his eyes. His smile was thin and fleeting. Bobby had been through a lot in his life, but he could not imagine his anguish.

"Tom, I'll ask you a lot of familiar questions," Bobby said. "Sorry, I need to ensure I miss nothing."

He took a deep breath and smiled. "Fire away; my life is an open book."

For the next 15 minutes, he confirmed the basics of the case.

"Is there anyone who would want to hurt you or your family? Any money issues?" Bobby explained that he had set up a timeline and viewed what little video information they had. Thomas did not know why Jessica would have left the class and gone in any direction but to his office. The food arrived, and as they ate, he talked about some of his memories of her and the family. How Jessica was funny, driven and naturally inquisitive. He paused twice, overcome by his emotions. He recovered quickly, though. The man was resilient and vigilant, still on a mission, as Bobby's comrades would say.

"Is there any chance she's still alive?" he asked Bobby, maintaining eye contact. Tears welled up behind his glasses. It was the ideal time to offer him closure and let him down gently.

Bobby knew, in most cases; 72 hours was the window to find a kidnap victim alive. He had every intention of lessening the poor man's expectations. However, looking into Tom's desperate and tortured eyes, he said, "There is always a chance, and if she is out there. I *will* find her."

Thomas removed his glasses and sat back, looking up at the ceiling, tears streaming down his face now. The two finished their lunch in silence. As they shook hands, he hugged Bobby. "Thank you for not giving up on her," his voice was uneven with emotion. "I thought you wanted to meet me just to say that it was hopeless. I have little money, but—" Bobby stopped him mid-sentence. Letting him know he was paid in full. Thomas smiled. "Let me at least get the check." He motioned to Darla, but Ernie, who had been cleaning a booth to their right, said.

"Your money's no good here, Mr. Grant." He shook Ernie's hand and Bobby's. "I'll be in touch," Bobby assured him. He left the restaurant as if granted a reprieve. Bobby was standing there, smiling a bit, when Ernie came up beside him. "You poor dumb bastard! Do you always promise your clients the impossible? I mean, the FBI and NYPD had no luck, but your gimpy, Jarhead ass is going to find her?"

Bobby smiled, "Marines are always up for the impossible, Gunny. You know that."

Ernie had completely misjudged him a few days ago. He smiled back and said, "Just let me know if you need help, Bobby. Now, what did you think of the Risotto?"

Bobby frowned. "It was, unfortunately, glorious!

THIRTEEN:

THE JETS STILL SUCK

B obby arrived at the Sons of Italy just as the fourth quarter began. The Jets were up by ten points over the much-hated New England Patriots. The room was buzzing with excitement.

"See," his dad was saying, "even the GOAT gets old, eventually." He had to agree. He missed a couple of passes high, and the Patsy's had to punt. The Jets' troubles began when they got the ball on their own thirty. After moving the ball to midfield, the new golden boy held the ball too long and was strip sacked. That was not good. He had watched this movie too often. The Jets are up, then some pivotal plays happen, and the Patriots jump right back into the game. He looked at the game clock, a little over 12 minutes left in the game. "10 points up, we got this one," Dad said, but Bobby was not sure if he was trying to convince us or convince himself.

"He's too old and slow. He's done," his brother replied.

The QB ran a brilliant play fake and hit the tight end twenty yards deep. Eleven minutes left. He then threw it to the end zone, and the safety jumped the route. The ball hit him in the chest, but he dropped it. A collective cry rattled the building. On the very next play, they covered the receivers deep.

Even though the QB could be timed with a sundial, he stepped up in the pocket, gained ten yards, and slid safely down.

"Shit!" yelled his father. On the next play, the NFL's senior ambassador threw a laser strike to the corner of the end zone. Touchdown. Suddenly, all the regulars in the club started switching their seats like baseball players and superstitions of athletes, donning their rally caps, hoping to stem the tide. The defense tackled the halfback immediately when the Patriots went for two and attempted an ill-advised screen to the flat. The game clock showed just over nine minutes remaining. After the kickoff, the Jets drove the field but settled for a field goal. Up by a touchdown, we thought. The game clock read one minute and 49 seconds. Everyone in the room knew that was more than enough time for the wily old pro.

"No way, not this time!" his brother Gio said to no one in particular. "We've got your ass!" The Pats stalled at the Jets' 40, fourth and eighth. He snapped the ball. The QB launched the ball downfield, incomplete. The entire room erupted. There was, of course, a late flag on the play. Roughing the passer, fifteen yards, automatic first down. The room strongly disagreed with the call. Screaming, cursing, flipping over chairs, calling both Belichick and the ref's mothers' terrible names, all mature stuff. The next play, naturally, The Pats scored a touchdown. They ran the same play for a two-point conversion, but it worked this time. The room was again in a state of shock. As the clock ran out on another Jets loss to the Patriots, Bobby left. No, he decided, that's it. He was done with the Jets, maybe even football.

"See you next week, Bobby?" his dad's neighbor asked. Who was he kidding? "You bet; Mr. Fricano, I'll be here."

FOURTEEN:

SHOOT THE MESSENGER

On Sundays, after the Jets loss, Bobby's Aunt Gina provided Sunday dinner. Even though Gina owned a diner and was Italian, they well knew that she could not cook, a potential problem when she hosted Sunday dinner. What Gina had was a professional cook named Lennox, who, besides his normal duties, prepared Sunday dinner for the Bocchini clan. He even delivered it to his parents' house at four pm every Sunday in a little Ford transit van. Gina purchased it a couple of years ago from a florist. The van was pink, and no matter how many times she cleaned it out, it still had a faint smell of roses. Given the circumstances, it could be worse. Now, Lennox was a splendid cook, had a sunny disposition, and could crank out food at an astonishingly high rate, though he knew nothing about Italian food. Everything was a little off; it all had an extra spicy component. His Mom had, from time to time, offered her advice, but in the end, it remains consistently Jamaican/Italian.

That Sunday, Lennox was sick with the flu. Bobby's mom was getting ready to pull out the leftovers from Saturday when his brother Anthony came up with a solution. "

"Hey, Bobby, what was the name of that joint you ate the other day?"

A feeling of dread came over Bobby.

"Didn't you say it was the best fettuccine you ever had?"

Suddenly, all eyes fell on Bobby. His mother's mouth hung open, her eyes wide with the perfect combination of rage and disbelief.

"The best?" she asked. Bobby backpedaled.

"I meant the best from a non-Italian."

His mother literally gasped. Anthony had a grin from ear to ear, knowing what he had started, loving the painful expression on his face. Later, Bobby would have to destroy him, of course, but now he was in full damage control mode.

"She's not Italian?" His mom asked.

"It's not even a woman," Anthony began, but Bobby brought his cane up behind him, hitting his brother in the balls. He doubled over on the sofa. Just then, his cell rang.

"Whoops, client call."

"Hello, Bobby Bocchini." he said, trying to extricate himself from the room.

"Bobby, it's Autumn." She sounded like she had been crying.

"Wait, let me hear you better," he said, going out onto the porch and giving his brother a threatening look with a throat-slashing gesture. He returned to a curled-up position and smiled. He hadn't been able to give him a clean shot; it merely glanced at the target area. Payback would be monumental for the little shit, but that would have to wait.

"Sorry, Autumn, go ahead." He walked out to the rental car Du jour, a brand-new Ford F250 pickup. This was his kind of vehicle, big, with lots of room to stretch out his legs. He would consider moving in if there was a bathroom.

"Say that again, Autumn," he said.

"Bobby, I have a letter that Jessica gave me. I thought it was only a school paper or something, but Bobby, it appears that she was tracking someone!"

"What do you mean by following someone?" he asked. "Doing surveillance on someone? I will come there."

"Oh, Bobby," she started, obviously upset. "How could I be so stupid? What if this had led to finding her earlier? I will never forgive myself!"

"Autumn, listen to me. We do not know what it is you have. And we are unsure of what contribution. It might have been seven years ago. So, for now, just relax. I will be there shortly."

When he arrived at Autumn's apartment, she met him at the door. Her eyes were red and puffy. She had obviously been crying.

"Bobby," she said and fell into his arms. "What have I done? What have I done? How could I have been so reckless?"

He helped her to the sofa and held onto her lovely face. "Listen to me; the best thing we can do right now is remain calm. May I see the letter?"

It was a couple of pages long, double-spaced. Cheap printer paper, as you would expect from a school's computer lab. Precisely as Autumn had described it. The letter recorded people's movements around the neighborhood. A sad smile crept across his face; Jessica really wanted to be a detective. It was all benign stuff, interesting only to a young child. It talked about people getting on and off the bus, ladies with extremely high heels, short dresses, and glittery make-up—probably hookers. Boys looking silly, with their pants low and showing their underwear. This made her chuckle a bit. Bobby could not agree more! Then it mentioned the "sad" man. She described him as old, but to someone Jessica's age, that could be a person in their thirties. She had written that he was not as tall as her dad. Thomas was six feet tall, so, call it five eleven or under. Reddish hair shaped like a half-moon.

"Did she mean sitting up on top of his head like that hideous Flock of Seagull's hairdo?" he asked aloud. "Or it could mean that he was balding."

"Male pattern balding?" Autumn asked.

"That could be in a semi-circle."

"That's true," she mentioned, taking pictures of a couple of people. Maybe she snapped a picture of the sad man.

"Autumn, did she have a camera with her normally?"

"I do not think so. She had a cell phone, though," she said. "I remember because her dad made sure she always had only the best. I think it was a Motorola or Samsung? It was green!" Autumn suddenly remembered.

"What kind of green?" he asked.

"You know that shiny acid green? She loved that color. She had a backpack that was the same color, and her tennis shoes, too. It was her signature color if a kid could have such a thing."

Bobby could not recall any reference to a phone in the police or FBI reports. They would have looked at that first if they could get in.

"She did not leave the phone at the school or anything. Did you have a Lost and Found?" She did not. Bobby called Thomas Grant and asked him if he knew anything about her phone.

"That was the first thing the police asked me," he told Bobby. "But, I remember, we ordered a special attachment for it. She called it a Fisheye lens. Clipped over the lens and improved zoom. Why are you asking about that?"

"I'm just following up on a lead." He refrained from telling him about the log.

His next call was to Sal. Bobby inquired about a green cell from seven years past. Sal laughed at him.

"Do you know how many missing items pass through here in a month, kid? Are you seriously asking about a phone lost seven years ago?" Sal laughed again.

"Look, I know it's a long shot, Sally, but could you at least cross-reference it in the system?" he asked.

His demeanor changed. "This is about Jessica's case?"

"Yes," he replied. "I'll have Getz look," he said.

"Bobby, I appreciate you taking this so seriously, and I know you well enough to be sure that you are running down every potential lead. Not all situations have a happy conclusion. Just keep that in the back of your mind. This was the most soul-crushing case I ever worked on."

He sighed. "Sal, I know where this will probably end up. Either to a shallow grave along a highway or, even worse, nowhere at all, but I promised Thomas Grant an answer. You know what I mean."

"Yeah, kid, I do, and I will let you know if we turn up anything."

"That is all I can ask for, Sal. Thanks," he said and hung up. It was getting late, and he had to pick up the surveillance on Nina Adams in the morning. Bobby said good night to Autumn; she suddenly put her arms around his neck and kissed him with intent. Then she stepped back.

"Oh my god, I am so sorry, Bobby! I am not sure what came over me." She was obviously embarrassed.

"Not to worry, Autumn. Women just find chubby Italian guys with canes irresistible." They burst into laughter. "It's the nicest thing that's happened to me in a while," he said.

"Yeah?" she asked in a whisper. "Absolutely," he said, gazing into those beautiful eyes. She leaned in again, her beauty and warmth enveloping him like a warm blanket. People overestimate the importance of sleep. He concluded. That's why they make coffee.

FIFTEEN:

THAT'S MATURE

B obby arrived home just after one am and got a solid five hours of sleep before being jolted awake by the alarm clock. He ran through the shower, shaved, and dressed in record time. He promised Walter that he would call him at 11 am to give him an update, not a call Bobby was looking forward to. Not only had he lost her one evening, but his suspicions might be correct. She had been to what sounded like a truly twisted nightclub, or rave, or whatever you wanted to call it. It all seemed so out of character, though Nina seemed smart, put together, and extremely accomplished. How does a woman of her stature fall into that kind of situation? He arrived across from Adam's house at 7:30 and saw Walter's Audi Q8 pull onto the street. Fifteen minutes later, Nina followed suit and started her day. Her day followed the same pattern as a week earlier. A large green drink, board meetings, etc.... Nina was at her meeting at the Met by 11:00, so he took that opportunity to grab a coffee and call Walter. He explained all that had transpired the week before, including the part about losing her on Wednesday night.

"Are you kidding?" Walter said. "How, in God's name, how did that happen?"

"Walter, I apologize, but it just isn't possible to prepare for every variable," he said. "Abandoning her car and taking a cab in the opposite direction is a very savvy move. It's more like a tradecraft. I simply did not see it coming."

"No, no, Bobby, I'm sorry," he said, regaining his composure. "Do you know where she went?" Bobby explained he located the driver and uncovered where she was taken to.

"Where?" Walter asked, short of breath. Bobby reported on his discoveries from The Palace. Walter got very emotional.

"I was afraid of that," he said, clearing his throat and trying his best to remain composed. "Thank you, Bobby. How much do I owe you?"

"Walter," he said, "I neither saw nor have any actual evidence that she entered the club."

"But you said—" Walter began.

"Walter, all I have are the recollections of a gin-soaked, flop house front desk clerk. Hardly credible, certainly not enough to come to any conclusions. I wanted to give you the latest update. Did she act strangely this weekend?" he asked.

"She was distant, not her normal on-vacation self. Does that mean anything?" Walter asked meekly.

"Not necessarily, Walter. Please wait before making any rash decisions or confronting her until I have a better idea of what is going on."

Walter sighed and said, "I want to speed this up somehow."

"That is a great idea, Walter. She may let her guard down. *If* she has something to hide."

Walter agreed to tell his wife he would leave for Hartford in the morning and would not be back until Thursday morning. Nina had an uneventful rest of her day. She returned home at 6:00 pm. Walter texted him that Nina was off to bed after 9:00, so Bobby returned home. He was sitting at his apartment watching Monday Night Football. The Steelers were killing the Browns; nothing new about that. Bobby wanted to call Autumn all day, but resisted the temptation. He read an article that stated women craved attention, not suffocation. His only manly wisdom came after dating for most of his adult life. "Don't smother them." Brilliant. So, he texted her instead, but with the "Whoops, I'm sorry, I thought I texted my mom" ruse. Your mother, he thought, how pathetic does that sound? Bobby was having second thoughts about all of it. He was not sure how smart, or even ethical, it was to have a relationship with someone in the middle of a case he was working on.

Make the mature choice, the right one. Just say, Autumn, I am afraid our involvement has been a mistake, and we should keep our relationship strictly professional.

"Hello," she answered. "Autumn, it's Bobby... Bocchini."

She laughed. "Well, thanks for clearing that up. Suddenly, all that manly resolve melted away like a snowball in Tampa.

"I was just thinking about you."

"Good, I was thinking about you, too." She laughed. OMG, he thought to himself, so much for the mature choice.

SIXTEEN:

THE MAKING OF A MONSTER

Michael Brady did not consider himself a monster, although most people would disagree.

He began life normally enough. His father was an electrician, and his mother was a dental hygienist. He grew up in the St. Albans section of Queens, graduated from high school, and planned to become an attorney, but never could quite get the hang of college. He got a job instead. Selling aluminum siding, then life insurance, never truly distinguishing himself in any of his endeavors. He became a fan of those late-night infomercials and can't miss investment schemes. First, he tried to buy houses with no money down, then dubious investments, eventually ending with a Ponzi scheme. They convicted him of operating a pyramid scheme that promised "ground floor investors triple digit returns." The court found him guilty and sent him to a minimum-security prison in upstate New York for five years. His father died in 2006 while Michael was serving his sentence. He never quite got over the fact that his father viewed him as a great disappointment. His mother bankrolled his business ventures with the proceeds from her husband's life insurance.

Fresh with funding, he tried his hand at day trading, and the result was entirely predictable. Picking the wrong stocks or selling them too early or late. It was extremely difficult to time the market, especially when relying on hunches. He lost half of the money his mother had given him. His last attempt at a legitimate business was a Hail Mary. He saw Blockbuster and other rental giants struggle against Redbox and started his own company. Empire Video Direct, Hollywood hits for the five boroughs. He bought 15 video rental machines and had them painted pink, his mother's favorite color. Purchased three small used cargo vans and hired two driverschnicians to fill and service them. He got all the machines placed outside smaller local groceries or bodegas. He filled them with various newer movies, and things seemed to look up. Like most first-time entrepreneurs, he fell victim to what the small business administration called "the triple double." When starting a new business, it took twice as much time, money, and expertise as most people think it would to get a business off the ground. Also, like many people, he failed to foresee the rise of video streaming services. The money from his mom ran low, which meant he could not keep up with the constant exchange of new movie titles, so fewer people were renting his DVDs. Then he paid his employees late, which led to turnover.

His mother, true to that sacred motherly bond, borrowed money from the bank with her house as collateral, the stress of which led her to having a stroke. Now Michael faced an additional problem: how to take care of his mother. Her stay at the hospital and the mounting medical bills pushed him to the breaking point. It forced him to shut down the company. The creditors repossessed two of his three vans and he sold twelve of his fifteen machines. Only keeping the three nearest to the small warehouse that he operated out of. It was in an alley across the street from Autumn's ballet studio. He was often spotted walking from machine to machine, rotating the DVDs, which by the end were Spanish language titles. This was when a curious young filmmaker took notice of him in the alley across the street and labeled him "The Sad Man."

SEVENTEEN:

AVALANCHE

(2014)

"**M**r. Brady, this is Robert Pearson from Garden State Mutual," the answering machine announced. "This is his fifth and final message. You and your family are now five thousand four hundred dollars in arrears, plus late fees. Because of the 90-day delinquency, we will foreclose on the property."

Michael had played back the message a second time. "What the fuck am I supposed to do now?" he asked as he sat alone in his empty warehouse. The money was gone, his business was bankrupt, and now he would have to move. What about his mom? He brought his mother home after her stroke and paid a day nurse while he worked, but he only had $50 left and needed to pay her in two days. They forced him to pay six months in advance for the warehouse space, but soon they would want their money too.

Michael called a slew of banks, finance companies, and government entities begging for a loan or help. However, his credit history, criminal record, and six-month waiting lists had stopped him cold. He needed a break, so he walked a few blocks to a shitty little bar to think and drown his sorrows. He was on his fifth PBR when he noticed a group in a booth at the end of the bar.

The bald man retrieved an envelope from his pocket and passed it to the person across from him. The man opened the envelope, and Michael saw it was full of cash.

"Who is that?" Michael asked the bartender.

"That is the devil. Do not even look his way."

"The devil? What do you mean?"

"He is a bad dude, a pimp, a loan shark, you name it."

A loan-shark? Michael thought. "What's his name?" Michael asked.

The bartender shook his head. "Sergei, something or other. He is a Russian."

Michael finished his beer and worked up his courage. He tentatively walked over to the booth and slid in opposite "the devil."

"Hi Sergei," Michael said. "My name is Michael Brady." He extended his hand to the Russian.

"I don't give a fuck who you are," the little man said. "I don't know you."

"The bartender said you may be able to assist a business owner who needs a short-term loan."

Sergei smiled, showing his crocodile smile highlighted by two gold-plated front teeth. "Why didn't you say so?" he replied. "Step into my office." He motioned to the men's room. As soon as he entered, another bigger guy grabbed Michael, shoved him headfirst into the wall, and punched him in the gut.

"Are you a cop? Are you wearing a wire?" Sergei asked, ripping open Michael's shirt.

"No, please stop!" Michael said as he gasped for breath. "Look, I own Empire Video around the corner. I'm in a pinch and find myself short on cash. I am expecting a large settlement next month," he said, lying. "And I need a little bridge money."

"Why not go to the bank?" Sergei asked.

"Banks don't like guys like me."

"What do you mean, like you?" Sergei asked.

"You know ex-cons." Michael exhaled.

"So," Sergei said, now relaxed, knowing that Michael was no threat. He wasn't a cop or a Fed. He was just another stupid American in over their head and desperate enough to borrow money from him. "You have those ugly pink video machines?" he asked, laughing. "The one with the old movies?"

Michael confirmed the gangster's accurate assessment with a simple, "Yep, that's me."

"What is this settlement you are expecting, and how much is it?"

Michael panicked a bit; he was not expecting the guy to do any fact-checking. "It's a medical malpractice settlement, and it's for four hundred thousand dollars." He lied again.

"How much do you need?" Sergei asked.

"Ten thousand should do it," Michael said. He considered asking for additional funds, but changed his mind as wasn't sure how he would pay back the $10K.

"Done," Sergei said happily. He grabbed Michael's hand, squeezed it hard, and looked him in the eyes. "If you miss a payment, I will cut off a finger. If you run, I will kill you and everyone you care about." Sergei gave Michael one final violent shake. "Meet me at the bar tomorrow at two pm."

The terms were simple. Michael owed them one thousand a week and a fifteen thousand balloon payment in two months. The bartender's reference to Sergei as the Devil finally made sense to Michael. Michael went back to sit on his barstool. Sergei and his crew got up and walked out of the bar. He slid the bartender a twenty-dollar bill and winked at Michael. "See you tomorrow."

After they were gone, the bartender reiterated his plea. "Listen, you do not want to take his money, trust me. You are making a Faustian mistake."

Michael twisted his face into a puzzled look. "What?" he asked.

The bartender shook his head. "Never mind, keep that twenty on the bar. You are going to need it."

EIGHTEEN:

MYSTERY MAN

Autumn and Bobby spoke on the phone for two hours the previous evening. It was amazing how simple conversation came early in a relationship. Wow, Bobby thought, am I in a relationship with her? Again, he thought, is it smart to get involved with someone who is part of his ongoing investigation? Too late for second thoughts now. Bobby liked her; he really liked her. He was determined not to overthink his stroke of good luck. When Walter's car rolled out of the driveway, it jolted Bobby back to reality.

Bobby had dropped off his rental last night and was in his own Hyundai today. Nina was unusually late this morning. By 10 am, Bobby had caught up on his emails and discussed the Alfredo incident as they came to know it in the family with Tony before Nina was ready to leave. Tony still thought it was hilarious, despite his bruised nether regions. He also checked in with Sal about Jessica's cell phone. No progress on that front. It was a long shot, Bobby realized. Nina had one addition to the schedule. She was on the committee planning the annual Met Gala, called Costume Institute Benefit. The event took place in early May, but they were well into the planned season. Which called for additional sub-committee meetings. He settled in, as this would normally be at least an hour. Bobby was about to go find a cup of coffee, but he hesitated for a moment. That was fortunate because after only 45 minutes, Nina emerged from the museum and hailed a cab. This time, both he and the taxi traveled in the same direction. The cabbie dropped her off at a diner ten blocks away. Unusual because Nina was far too healthy to frequent such a place. Bobby parked the car across the street and got out. He observed Nina meet with a man.

Oh no, looks like Walter's fears are coming true, Bobby thought. He pulled out his phone and snapped a couple of pictures. He made the tactical decision to go inside the diner. Nina was sitting at a booth by the window. Bobby took a position at the corner of the counter and ordered coffee. The man was younger, approximately six feet, two inches tall, with dark hair. He had a military bearing, and Bobby could not hear what they were saying. It certainly did not seem like a romantic discussion. Their tones were even, with no smiles or laughter. It seemed business-like. The customer next to Bobby paid for his tab and left. Bobby slid onto the open stool to get slightly closer to hear them. Bobby's back was to them, and despite his multiple injuries from 9/11, his hearing was perfect.

"Are you saying you can't arrange it?" Nina was saying.

The man chuckled. "You are a woman who knows what she wants," the man said in a heavy European accent. "The demand for such an item is high, and the bidding will be fierce."

"Can you get me in or not?" Nina asked.

"Anything's possible," the man whispered, "for the right price."

At least it was not another man, thought Bobby. Not sure how much consolation that will be, though.

"Call me when you have a date." Nina said, then she produced a cheap-looking phone. There was the number she said as she looked at a post it note on the back of the phone. Bobby had a clear view of everything from the counter mirror. A burner phone, he thought. Well, that makes sense. Bobby paid his bill and started to exit the diner just after Nina excused herself and headed to the restroom. When Bobby stood, the European man was beside him.

"Why do you listen to our conversation, fat ass?" he asked. "The cat's curiosity can be dangerous," he sneered.

"I was just leaving," Bobby said, standing to his full six feet four inches in height. "You remember what I say, Cyka?" Bitch in Russian. Bobby had the urge to smash his cane across the guy's skull, but he did not need any undue attention.

"Excuse me," he said as he approached the door. Bobby got to his car as Nina hailed a cab back to the museum. What the hell have you gotten yourself into, Nina? Bobby thought as he followed the cab. He noticed Nina was once again talking on a cell phone. He could not make out which one it was, but the knowledge that there was one was troubling.

HOUSE OF CARDS

(2014)

Michael's house of cards crumbled shortly after borrowing the money. Without a steady income, catching up was hopeless for him. He was using the principle to make weekly payments to Sergei, with the balloon payment nearing. "I will kill you and everyone you love." Sergei's words kept replaying in his mind. "Everyone!" The only person Michael had was his sickly mother. If he ran, would Sergei find his mom in whatever nursing facility the state placed her in and kill her? Absolutely, he thought. He was, as advertised, the devil.

Michael's uncle Richard had left his mother a cabin two hours from the city. The "cabin" was little more than a rusty old trailer outside of Lake Haven, Pennsylvania. He and his dad had used it to go fishing and hunting back in the day. The location was extremely remote but had a well and propane for heat. It also had a generator for electricity. When the day nurse arrived, he decided to take a day trip to see it. "Mom, I'm leaving town for the day, but I'll be back before five." His mother looked up and smiled.

"Okay," she said weakly. "See you then."

"I will be back later this afternoon," he told Anna, the latest in a lengthy string of caregivers, each slightly less qualified than the last. She nodded, looking up briefly from her cell phone.

He crossed over the Hudson and jumped on eighty-seven north, then Route 6 West, then 84 West. One hundred fifteen miles and two hours later, he pulled up in front of the trailer. It was smaller than he remembered. Michael tried to mortgage it, but they deemed it almost worthless. Then, he tried to sell it again, but no one wanted it. He unlocked and opened the door, and dank and stale air assaulted his nostrils. "Holy shit," he said aloud. "No wonder nobody wants this piece of junk." He opened the windows to let a little fresh air in. The crank on the casement window was rusted completely shut. A horrible old carpet was full of mildew from the dampness; the ceiling showed weather circles from a leak in the roof. He dreaded what might be in the fridge. It had literally been years since anyone had been inside. His plan was to bring his mom here while he figured out what to do next, but it was not a workable solution. This would be a death sentence for his mom in her current state.

As he drove back to the city, a feeling of gloom overtook him. Michael was an atheist, refusing to consider the possibility of a divine entity despite his parents' efforts to take him to church. It seemed like a ridiculous notion to him. So even now, in his darkest hours, he couldn't or would not bring himself to ask God for help. So, if God were out of the equation, then maybe he could make a deal with Sergei, the devil. Because while he didn't believe in God, or angels, he knew without a doubt that evil was real.

TWENTY:

NINA'S PAST

Nina-Adams, on the surface, had it all. A tall, beautiful brunette. Her clothes were immaculate, stylish, and expensive. She had graduated from Vassar with a degree in economics and a minor in finance. She met her husband Walter in a suite at Yankee Stadium. Merrill Lynch had sponsored the event. Nina was working for them at the time as an emerging markets specialist. Walter, six years her senior, was more than smitten. He fell in love at first sight, clear to all who saw them meet. Walter managed the finances of wealthy New Yorkers and was well-regarded. He was a VIP guest at the game. Nina was familiar with him, but only by reputation. They hit it off, and a rapid, energetic courtship ensued. Walter, at every turn, tried to impress while wooing her. Romantic trips, jewelry, lavish dinners. All the attention paid off. They were engaged and had been married for eleven years. It had been a fairy tale for Nina, but as we all know, fairy tales often have dark beginnings, and Nina's beginning was just that. She grew up in Pittsburgh, Pennsylvania, and her parents were far from a high-powered couple. Nina's mother was a Nurse, and her dad was an Allegheny County Firefighter. They loved each other, and they loved Nina. She was especially close to her father, like most little girls. She always felt safe when she was with him. A tragic turn happened in Nina's life when her parents both died in a car accident on New Year's Eve, 1990. They were coming home from a party when a drunk driver crossed the center line and collided with their car head-on. It killed both instantly. Ten-year-old Nina went to live with her aunt and uncle in Baltimore. When her aunt and uncle divorced a few years later. Nina stayed with her uncle, as he was her blood relative. The next eight years were far from a fairy tale. Her alcoholic uncle began molesting her shortly after her aunt left. He asserted power over her. She believed he was the only one she had left, and, without him, she would be abandoned and isolated in this inhospitable world. He blamed his sickness, his perversion, on the impressionable little girl. However, Nina would eventually break free of her uncle and have him arrested. She remembered vividly the day the Baltimore Police showed up at his house. For all his abusive behavior towards her and his tough talk. When the police came, he folded like a cheap suit. Eventually, he took the coward's way out and committed suicide before they put him in prison. Nina spent years restoring her life, but the years of abuse spilled over into her personal life. On the surface, she seemed well-adjusted, successful, and happy, but the deep scars on her psyche took her to dark places. In college, she always dated the wrong guy, the bad boy. Her relationships were brief, physical, and often abusive. Random partners, and dangerous places, all of which left her empty inside. In her junior year, Nina's new roommate, Caroline, a beautiful young ASL student, changed her life. They spend hours talking and crying together. She eventually talked Nina into speaking to a counselor. Even going with Nina to lend moral support. After years of arduous work, Nina emerged triumphantly and took her life back. Five years after that, she met Walter. She was very honest and upfront with him. She explained all that had happened to her. His reaction was not what she had expected. Instead of being appalled and ending the relationship, as she had feared. Tears rolled down his cheeks, and he gently took her by the hands and knelt beside her. "I am so deeply sorry for what happened to you, my beautiful girl. If the pervert were still alive, I would kill him." He exhibited an anger Nina had never seen in him. "And what would that accomplish?" Nina asked. "You're right, of course," Walter replied. "How about this? I will consider it my life's work to make you happy and bring nothing but love and light into your life." They were married the following April. An opulent affair attended by dozens of New York's blue blood and corporate aristocracy. True to his word, Walter had whisked Nina away on their honeymoon to the city of Light. You know what they say about April in Paris.

TWENTY-ONE:

INTERPOL?

Bobby snapped photos of the man with Nina. The following morning, he saw Sal.

"Could I ask a favor of you?"

"Depends on the favor and how much hot water it's going to get me in," Sal said with a smile.

"I have a picture of a foreign national that I would like to identify," Bobby said.

"Is he associated with the Jessica Grant case?" Sal asked, eyebrows raised.

"Maybe," Bobby lied.

"Our stuff, or Interpol?"

"Both?" Bobby said sheepishly.

Sal stared at him for a long second. "I'll see what I can do," he said.

It was just a hunch, but cases have turned on less, Bobby thought as he walked back to his car. Nina might be into something shady. There was little doubt in Bobby's mind now that she was. This guy might have a rap sheet.

When Walter arrived home the following day, he called Bobby, inquiring about what had happened when he was gone. Bobby explained what he had seen, and Walter breathed unevenly.

"Do you think he was her lover?" he asked.

"Absolutely not!" Bobby replied.

"Then who is he?" Walter asked, bewildered.

"I'm not sure. It was like a business meeting. I got a photo of him, and I am having it checked with the NYPD and Interpol."

"Interpol?! Did I not mention the need for discretion?" Walter replied.

"Relax, Walter. His source is very discreet, and he does not know who you or Nina are."

Walter let out a cleansing breath. "Well, that is a relief. What is next?

"Well," Bobby said. "If I can find out who this guy is, maybe I can reverse engineer what the hell is going on here."

Bobby followed Nina for the rest of the day with nothing unusual occurring. He wondered how Walter could keep up his normal interactions with Nina knowing, or at least thinking he knew, what was going on. He is one cool customer, but I suppose those high-powered investment guys must have ice water flowing through their veins, Bobby thought.

The following day was uneventful. Nina kept to her schedule, but even from a distance, Bobby noticed that her actions and demeanor were different. She did not have the same confident stride or attitude. Nina seemed preoccupied, even agitated. It was as though the weight of the world was on her shoulders. I suppose infidelity will do that, Bobby thought. Wait, have I really found evidence of or truly witnessed anything that proves that is happening? No, he concluded. Everything is circumstantial. It certainly looks bad, but it would not stick in a court of law. We should view everyone as innocent until proven otherwise.

Still, he had a bad feeling about it. He tried to replay the pieces of the conversation he had heard in his mind. It sounded like she was trying to purchase something, but what? Drugs? He wondered. No, he thought. The one thing he could unequivocally say was that Nina was neither a junkie nor a drug dealer. Okay, nothing drug-related, then what? Diamonds, artwork? The Russian, or whoever he was, said that everything has a price and one can get anything for the right amount. He returned to art, perhaps because of the word "bidding" or because he watched *The Thomas Crown Affair* recently. That Brosnan guy was so smooth, with women, with men, hell probably with farm animals. What are you trying to buy, and why would you be dealing with some piece of Euro-trash? Bobby's phone rang. Autumn's number scrolled across the tiny screen. "Why, hello darling" he said, trying to channel his inner-Brosnan.

Autumn paused for a second. "Are you feeling alright, Bobby?"

So much for smoothness, he thought.

TWENTY-TWO:

LET'S MAKE A DEAL

(2014)

The balloon payment was due in a week. Michael could not eat. He barely slept for an hour or two per night. He had visibly aged ten years. His once-dark hair was turning increasingly gray. Even his mother noticed the difference as she weaved in and out of lucidity.

"Michael, honey," she asked. "What is wrong? Did you fail that math test?" She was replaying a memory from twenty years ago. "Don't worry," she said. "Your father will be home soon, and he can help you work through it. Don't worry." She slipped back to sleep. If only, Michael thought. Despite being dead for years, the thought of his father calmed him. What would his dad do? He would try to negotiate a solution. Worth a shot.

Michael entered the bar. Sergei and one of his goons were sitting in his office, the booth at the very back of the building, close to the restrooms and the door to the alley.

"Ah, Mikhail," Sergei said. "Sit down, have a drink. This was his favorite day of the year. The day when his customers pay off their loans. That is why you see me, right?"

"About that," Michael said. "I have run into a bit of a delay."

"A delay?" Sergei replied, his entire demeanor changing. "What sort of delay are we talking about? You did not get the settlement check?" Sergei's tone was low and ominous. He leaned closer now, his breath stinking of alcohol and cigarettes. "Did we not discuss the terms of your agreement?"

Michael wanted to scream and tell him there was no settlement, but he understood that would summon not only his demise, but his mom's too. "I just need more time," Michael said. Sergei nodded to his henchman, and he pulled Michael out of the booth and down the hallway. He elbowed Michael in the solar plexus, knocking all the air out of him so he could not scream. The bartender turned his head and shut his eyes, knowing what was happening. The goon virtually threw Michael into the alley.

"There is no more time, you little shit!" Sergei exclaimed. Michael tried to stand, but the henchman thrust his knee up into Michael's groin. The wave of pain and nausea drove Michael to his knees. "Tomorrow! All my money, or your mother, loses a finger!" Sergei's phone rang. "Da," he said, screaming. With each word, he became more agitated. He pressed the end button and kicked Michael in the ribs out of frustration. "It seems our delivery boy got himself killed and his truck impounded!" Sergei spat. "That motherless fuck! We need another way to transport the merchandise. Suddenly Sergei smiled as an alternative plan took shape. Mikhail," he said, helping Michael to his feet. "You have a van, right?"

"Yes, yes, I do," Michael said, his breath finally refilling his lungs.

"How would you like to get an extension on your loan? The devil laughed.

TWENTY-THREE:

TRAPPED

(2014)

Michael awoke with a start early the next morning. His entire body was hurting. Michael was sure his ribs were the very least cracked. He noticed swelling and bruising in his groin area. He got himself quietly into the bathroom to assess the damage. His eye had a hideous purple bruise, and his entire body, battered and beaten from head to toe. A ray of light appeared at the tunnel's end for the first time. Whatever they wanted him to haul, he would do it. Drugs, guns. He really didn't care if it kept him from a beating, or worse. A woman arrived to look after his mother before she woke up. He had been told to meet Sergei's henchman at Michael's warehouse at eight am, which he did. Michael got the keys and backed the van out. Nick, the henchman, was a man of few words.

"Drive," he said, and handed Michael a piece of paper. They drove to what looked like an abandoned strip mall. Nick ordered Michael to pull around to the back door. "Keys," Nick said, and Michael obliged. "Out of the van," Nick said, and once again, Michael did as he was told. Nick knocked at the entrance, and two other men who could have been carbon copies of good old Nick greeted them. Each with an equally charming personality.

"Good morning, Mikhail! Sergei said happily. He acted as if he hadn't almost killed him the day prior.

"Good morning," Michael said.

"Thank you for your help," Sergei said, as if Michael had a choice. "Let's get you all loaded up."

The room they entered looked like it may have been a freezer or meat locker at one point. To Michael's surprise, the "merchandise" was not drugs, stolen electronics, or guns. When they opened the door, there were six young women. Their ages ranged from perhaps fourteen to eighteen, he thought. Most of them were Hispanic or Asian. They all appeared to be drugged and were barely lucid.

"What the hell is this?" Michael asked.

"This Michael is your cargo; this is the only reason you and your whore of a mother are still alive," Sergei said. "Or do you have all of his money?"

"I can't do this," Michael said. "You can and you will," Sergei replied. "By the way," he continued, "I have a woman at your house looking after your mother. We gave the nurse the day off. Consider it as insurance for doing an excellent job. Michael realized he had absolutely no choice. Oh, and one more thing, Mikhail. If anything goes wrong, even if it's not your fault, Das Vandana momma. So please, drive carefully."

They instructed Michael to pull down a dead-end street several blocks from the nearest subway station. There was an odd concrete structure. He wondered if it was an old bunker or fallout shelter. Sergei's man leaned against a building at the alley's entrance. He pulled out a cigarette and lit it. Must be a lookout, Michael thought. Sergei's henchmen helped the girls exit through the van's side door. The bunker appeared deserted except for the new padlock. The man produced a key, unlocked it, and opened the door. A waft of stale air flowed out of the opening.

"Bring them inside," said the henchman. Following the henchman's instructions, Michael did as he was told. They descended a long flight of concrete stairs. Michael heard trains.

"What is the place? He asked. The henchman smiled.

"You Americans are such hypocrites! Your fancy hotels needed the Black workers, but didn't want them to be seen by the hotel guests. So, they created these servant access passages." Michael was unaware of its existence.

They walked five blocks in the near darkness, only illuminated by a small flashlight held by the henchman. One girl fell on the uneven surface and got slapped and pulled to her feet. Finally, he saw an exit ahead. They climbed up the stairs. He knocked, and a janitor opened the door. They were in the hotel. He could plainly see they directly took the girls to service elevators and that they tipped the hotel staff to allow them access. People walked by, ignorant of the situation.

Over the next several months, Michael helped deliver girls to various spots around the city and one trip to Boston. Eventually, Sergei explained Michael could wipe out the rest of his debt by helping increase the product on the supply side. It was disturbing how the Russians referred to the girls in business terms, regarded as a mere commodity, like light bulbs or toilet paper. Michael became numb to it. Any shred of human decency was gone. In fact, he became an expert in abduction. Michael's first taste of success came after Sergei referred to him as his rainmaker. It was at this moment that Michael encountered Jessica Grant. He noticed her looking at him from the ballet studio window. One day, he noticed she was following him. He strolled toward his warehouse. It was there he deployed his fail-proof method. As he opened the door, he allowed a small dog to escape.

"Oh no, Michael feigned alarm! Lucky, get back here!" Jessica dropped her phone and caught the puppy, not wanting it to run into the street.

"Thank you!" Michael smiled. "That was a close one."

She attempted to return the dog to Michael, saying, "Here you go. After letting the dog out, he grabbed a box of videos by the door.

"Sorry, my hands are full. Could you set him down here?" he asked as he opened the door again. "Sure!" Jessica said, completely disarmed by the puppy, as most of his young victims were. She walked inside his warehouse, unaware of the danger.

"Do you like puppies?" Michael asked, stepping aside to allow her entry.

"Who doesn't?" Jessica replied. Michael glanced around to ensure no one was watching. Who doesn't? Michael thought as an evil smirk flashed across his face.

TWENTY-FOUR:

CAPTURED

(2014)

Once Michael closed the door, he immediately applied a cloth soaked in chloroform to Jessica's nose and mouth. She had tried to scream and break away, but she was fifty pounds, no match for a full-grown man. She went limp, and Michael placed her on a cot. He returned to the parking lot to survey the area. You cannot be too careful, he thought. Four windows overlooked the alley. Michael knew that most buildings in the area were vacant. He picked up her backpack and a fancy-looking phone. He wiped down the phone and tossed it in a dumpster. Wait, he thought, can they track these things? He took the battery out. Afterward, he would reinstall the battery and dump it far away. Jessica was waking up, so Michael dosed her again with chloroform. Later that evening, he put Jessica in the van and took her to the abandoned storefront that functioned as Sergei's staging area for distributing his "merchandise."

Sergei greeted Michael as he brought the sleeping girl in. "What have you brought me today, Mikhail?" Sergei said warmly. His smile turned into a mask of rage and horror at the sight of the sleeping girl. "You idiot!" he said, slapping Michael across the face. "Haven't you seen the news!?" He pushed Michael into the office where the local news was on.

"This evening, the NYPD is asking for your help in finding this seven-year-old girl." There was a picture of Jessica. "Police say she left her dance studio around 4:30 today but never reached her father's office a few blocks away," the newscaster continued. "At this hour, an extensive search is underway. If you have any information, please call the number at the bottom of your screen. The little girl's family is offering a ten-thousand-dollar reward for any information that would lead to her safe recovery."

Sergei was seething. "What the fuck were you thinking?" he growled.

"She is just another kid, another piece of merchandise," Michael said, looking confused.

"She," Sergei exhaled slowly, trying not to have a stroke. "Is not! A little blonde, white girl? Her family and the entire NYPD are searching for her. She is not some anonymous runaway or crackhead no one will miss! They will tear this city apart looking for someone like her! Eliminate her immediately!" They both realized that Jessica was awake. Quickly, they injected her with a powerful tranquilizer, and she fell into a deep sleep. "Get rid of her and not anyplace in the city," Sergei said.

Michael placed the child back in the van. He drove to his house to check on his mother. He got her settled and gave her an over-the-counter sleep aid. Michael had two options. He could obey Sergei and dispose of her, or take the girl to a man who trafficked women. They might pay for a young white girl, he thought. Especially to those perverts in Asia or the Middle East. But if Sergei finds out, he will kill me, he thought. He put the van in reverse and backed onto the street. He drove west out of the city and toward Pennsylvania. There are a lot of deep lakes and dense forests in PA, he thought as a light rain began to fall.

TWENTY-FIVE:

NEEDLE IN A HAYSTACK

Bobby's alarm sounded at six am. He had given up rotating rental cars. It was expensive and overly cautious. Instead, he just switched with his dad. Now, instead of the electric Blue Hyundai, Bobby was driving a 2019 silver Ford Fusion. There were thousands of them floating around the city. If it was not invisible, it was nearly so. It had not been a simple transaction. Italians are extremely patriotic. His father, born in Italy, lived in the United States for almost fifty years. He considered it somehow wrong to drive a foreign car. Unless, of course, it had been an Italian car. That would be all right. Bobby persuaded his dad it was just temporary. Also, they had designed the Hyundai in California, engineered it in Michigan, and assembled it in Alabama. It was an American car. The tide turned after he offered to take his dad out for pizza. He was sitting across from Nina's house when his phone rang.

"You are one lucky SOB," said Sal on the other end.

"Why is that?" Bobby asked.

"Because I have not one, not two, but three green early-model cell phones in his office."

"Really?" Bobby replied in astonishment.

"When can you stop by?" Sal asked.

"Not sure. Can I call you later?"

"Yeah, no problem."

"Sal, wait," Bobby interjected, before his old boss could hang up. "Anything from Interpol yet?"

Sal chuckled. "Only one miracle a day, kid." Then he was gone. It was unlikely that one of the phones belonged to Jessica and had any value.

"You just never know," he whispered as Nina pulled out of the driveway. She made it to her initial meeting promptly, but paused when she exited her car. She had picked up her cell. Bobby could tell it was her burner phone. She immediately turned and got back into her car, heading east. Bobby picked up the tail, leaving three cars behind her. She arrived at the same diner that she had met before. There waiting was a different man with whom she had met the last time. Bobby refrained from entering because of being noticed the previous week. Bobby peered through the telephoto lens of his camera, trying to read Nina's lips, but he could not. He could see that it surprised her when the man handed her something. Was it a picture, a piece of paper? Bobby could not tell from this distance. Nina slowly nodded her head and stood to leave. He said something to her, and she nodded before leaving the restaurant. She drove to the Met for her second meeting a little early. Bobby noticed she appeared worried. He snapped another shot. She walked inside for her gala meeting, according to the schedule. Her visit would last 90 minutes. Plenty of time to stop by and see if Sal has the "acid green" needle in the haystack, he thought.

"Who was the new guy" Bobby asked himself. He looked completely different. From his suit to his demeanor. "What the hell is going on now, Nina?"

TWENTY-SIX:

PHONES, PIZZA AND NAMATH

Bobby called ahead, and Sal was waiting for him at the station. They entered a conference room close to the lobby.

"Okay, kid," Sal said. "As requested, here are three green smartphones." Bobby looked at them. He ruled out the first one because it was an iPhone. Bobby rejected the second smartphone because of its broken screen. "Shit, let's hope it isn't this one," Sal said. Bobby picked up the third phone and hit the power button. Nothing. He looked back at Sal.

"You didn't charge the phone?" Bobby asked.

"Sorry, Bobby, as you can see, it has one of those older charging ports. No one in the station has one of those anymore."

"Okay, can I take this? I might still have an old cord at the office,"

"It is all yours, kid; just sign this form." Bobby did and stood to leave. "You think the Jets have a chance on Sunday?" Sal asked.

"We are playing the Browns; they suck almost as much as we do."

"There's always hope," Bobby said, lacking conviction. "Did I ever tell you about the time I met Namath?" Bobby had heard the story a hundred times. He desperately wanted to avoid hearing the story again. He had to get back to Nina. Desperately, he wanted to invent an excuse to see Autumn. Most anything, in fact, but this story! Instead of vocalizing any of this, he said "Do tell," deciding to indulge his friend and mentor.

Sal said he was out running errands with the old man. Hanging out with him alone was rare, because he had five siblings.

"He took me to his favorite pizza shop, John's of Bleecker Street. He also liked Arturo's, but John Sasso, the owner, had come from Naples, so somehow, it felt like family. Anyway, we go in and sit down, and we see him. Joe Willie Namath, in the flesh! The old man could not believe it. I was too young to remember Superbowl III, but to this day, it is still an enormous deal to Jet's fans. I got up and went to Namath's table; My dad told me not to bother the great man, but I thought, what the hell? The waiter attempted to shoo me away, but Namath called me over. Joe smiled that toothy grin we knew him for and said, 'I don't know about that,' showing that southwestern Pennsylvania humility. 'Is your dad here?' he asked. My dad walked up behind me and said, 'Mr. Namath, we're sorry to interrupt your lunch.' 'No problem,' Joe said. Then he took off his Superbowl ring, handing it to me 'Try this on.' Naturally, it was huge on his ten-year-old fingers. He laughed. His dad held the ring for just a second and handed it back to Joe. 'Thank you,' his dad said. We went back and finished our lunch. Joe signed a napkin for us and shook the old man's hand on the way out. He asked us to watch his new TV show, *The Waverly Wonders*. We assured him we would. That autograph was his dad's prize possession until the day he died." Sal's eyes welled up.

"Now, it lives in an expensive frame behind Sal's desk. Anyway," Sal continued, "I hope the phone helps. Figuring out the passcode can be tricky. The manufacturers are not too keen on helping unlock them. Privacy and all that."

"First things first, I am going to change it up and take it to see if Jessica's father can identify it," Bobby said. "Who knows? Perhaps he even knows the code."

"Sure, Sal said. And the Jets might just win the Super Bowl this year." They both laughed at that one.

TWENTY-SEVEN

CLOSER

The day was uneventful for Nina. She was back home by 5:30. Walter's text confirmed that he and his wife were staying in. Bobby called Thomas Grant and asked him to meet at Ernie's diner around 6:15. He agreed, so Bobby called Autumn and invited her to meet him there at 7:00 for a quick bite.

She was a little standoffish at first. Saying something about how a bull gets what he wants, and then, bang, he's onto the next heifer. She tried to play it off as a joke, but he had been married long enough to realize she was completely serious. Bobby did not have time for this. He was working on not one, but two tough cases. But Autumn was also the best relationship Bobby had been in. "I'm sorry, Autumn," "I am afraid I have been working too hard between these two cases."

"I accept your Mea culpa," she said. Bobby promised to never take her for granted and make it up to her. Her mood brightened as she hung up to get ready.

When Bobby arrived at the diner, Thomas eagerly waited for him at a booth to fill him in. Bobby had swung by his office and picked up an old phone charger that fit the green phone.

"Thomas, I am going to show you something, but I don't want you to get too excited, okay?"

"Sure," Thomas agreed. Bobby produced the green phone from his pocket, and Thomas's eyes filled with tears. "Is that Jessica's phone?" he whispered. His voice choked with emotion. "Where did you find it?"

"First things first," Bobby said, "Can you verify that this is indeed Jessica's phone?" Thomas took the phone, cradling it gently in his hands as if it were as fragile as glass.

"Why is it so dusty?" Thomas asked.

"They dusted it for fingerprints," Bobby said. Thomas looked carefully and tried to turn it on, but the charge Bobby gave it on the short ride from the office did not bring it back to life.

"It certainly looks like hers," Thomas continued in a voice that sounded small and weak. Bobby asked Ernie if he could plug the phone in behind the counter, which he did. Bobby briefed him on the notes found at the Ballet studio. He made sure not to lay any blame on Autumn for not catching it sooner. Instead, saying that they had somehow missed it in the initial investigation. After fifteen minutes of charging, the phone still showed no signs of life.

"I'm afraid the battery is dead. I'll visit a phone store tomorrow for help," Bobby said. "In the meantime, do you have any idea what her passcode might be?" Thomas thought for a moment and gave Bobby three four-digit numbers to try: Jessica's birthday, her mom's, and his birthday. Bobby noticed Autumn's arrival through the window reflection. He assured Thomas he would be the first to know if he could get the phone up and running. Carefully, he handed the phone back to Bobby.

"If they prove it to be Jessica's, can I have it back?" Thomas asked.

"For the moment, it is potential evidence, but as soon as they can release it, I will move heaven and earth to get it back to you," Bobby replied. Thomas smiled faintly, thanked him, stood, and walked out of the diner.

Autumn walked over to the booth and kissed Bobby.

"Well, hello to you as well!" Bobby said happily.

Ernie came over with a couple of menus and ice water.

"Was that the little girl's phone?" Ernie asked.

"I'm not sure yet," Bobby said. "I need to start the thing and find the right passcode."

They had a nice dinner. Bobby stayed away from anything Italian, not sure his mother's heart could take another assault on her cooking prowess. That reminded him he had to punish his brother Tony excruciatingly. You know what they say about payback? he thought.

"Earth to Bobby," Autumn said. "Where did you go just now? You had a distant expression, followed by this devious grin. It was a little unsettling." Bobby explained the Alfredo incident with his mother. Autumn laughed wholeheartedly, a warm, beautiful laugh. It brought color to her cheeks and highlighted her perfect teeth.

After dinner, he walked back to Autumn's apartment. It was a beautiful fall evening. The leaves were turning, and there was just a hint of cooler weather. It was a perfect evening, and it only got better as the night progressed.

TWENTY-EIGHT:

SURPRISE

The tears streamed down Michael's face. "Mom, don't go, Mom!" He knew she had passed in her sleep. Her suffering was over.

"I don't know what happened," Jessica said sadly and fearfully. For seven years, she managed the woman's care. "I'm sorry." Seven years had passed, but Michael still remembered his intention of killing Jessica and disposing of the body. A bit of humanity remained. He simply could not do it. Kill an innocent child? He also could not set her free. The moment he arrived back home early the next morning, he had a sudden realization.

Michael busily began securing his mother's house. He added a partition and boarded the bedroom windows in the back of the house. Luckily, the house was in a dilapidated neighborhood facing the woods at the end of the street. This made it secluded. He applied chains to the girl's leg. He would remove them at night and confine her to a room. Each morning, he would chain her in his mom's room to care for her. By this point. Michael's mother had lost ground to dementia. She fully accepted that the child was Michael's daughter. Jessica tried to escape many times, leading to several severe beatings. Jessica believed Michael when he said that the next time she tried to escape would be her last. He even upped the ante by saying that his associates would kill her entire family. Should she try again? Slowly, she accepted her fate. No one came for her, and she simply could not comprehend why. Years passed, and she became attached to the older woman. So, when she shed tears for the woman's passing, they were real and heartfelt. Oddly, she thought of the old woman as her grandmother.

Michael now had a big problem. He would have to either have the authorities take his mother's body or dispose of it. A death, even one from natural causes, would bring the police. He could not bear the thought of not giving his mother a proper burial. The last step would be to eliminate Jessica. She was now fourteen and her story had faded from the news cycle. Sure, you had the occasional "what happened to Jessica Grant" news pieces or the odd podcast, but mostly, the world moved on. Over the years, Michael had gained contacts of his own in the trafficking business. He could easily sell her to one of them. He would have to be careful. If Sergei found out that he had not only disobeyed his command to dispose of her all those years ago, but then sold her to a competitor... well, Michael knew how that would end. So, Michael picked up one of his burners and made the call. The exchange would happen at midnight at Michael's warehouse. The Armenians would gladly take the girl, no questions asked.

He drugged Jessica's diet coke and waited for it to kick in. Michael tore down the partitions and boards from the windows. He gathered what few pieces of clothing and personal items Jessica had and put them in garbage bags. Then he loaded Jessica and the bags into the van. When he arrived at the warehouse, he pulled into the building. Michael bound and gagged Jessica and left her in the van. He kept his mom's old car at his building and drove back to the house. He gave the place the once over and called the authorities to report his mother's death. Within the hour, both the coroner and the police had arrived. They found a man whose grief was genuine. He had obviously cared for his mother well and, after a cursory discussion with the police, the coroner took the body to the morgue. Michael would have to call in the morning and make the arrangements, but first, he had to meet the Armenians in a few hours. He sat in the suddenly empty and quiet house, exhausted by the emotional toll and physical exertion. He fell into a deep, dreamless sleep.

TWENTY-NINE:

ALL ABOUT THE CODE

Bobby had already showered and shaved when he got a text from Walter. Nina was under the weather today. She would be at home. Bobby sighed. I wish I had known that a little earlier; he thought. A few more hours of sleep would have been helpful. Se la vie. It would allow him to get to the AT&T store earlier. Bobby headed out after getting dressed. He had to return his dad's car today, but since he had extra time, he stopped by his aunt's diner for breakfast.

The moment Gina saw him at the booth, she made a beeline for him. After the mandatory hug and kiss, she asked, "How is the big case going?"

"Which one?" he mistakenly replied.

"You have another big case?" Her excitement was palpable.

"Well, it's actually a missing person." Bobby regretted it instantly because she had planted herself in the opposite seat. Gina, by nature, immediately imagined the more lurid end of the spectrum.

"Missing wife? Murder for Hire?"

"You know, Angie, you watch way too much true crime TV," Bobby gently chided her. "Anyway, you know I can't talk about his clients." Had he told her about the Jessica Grant case, he would never have gotten rid of her or gotten his breakfast.

"You're no fun. Is it a crime that I am interested in his nephew's life?" she asked incredulously.

"Not at all," he said. "But we both know if I sold insurance, you wouldn't be nearly as inquisitive."

"Don't be fresh," she said and playfully slapped his cheek. What do you want for breakfast? She asked as she stood.

"Surprise me," Bobby said. Playfully, she stuck her tongue out and turned back towards the counter. He took out the green cell phone from his jacket pocket. His cousin Nico appeared and poured him coffee.

"Wow," he said, "look at that antique! Geez, Bobby, I'd say you need an upgrade!"

"It isn't mine. It's from a case I am working."

"That looks like the old Samsung we used to use for on-call and our delivery drivers." Nico said. Angie appeared with breakfast.

"What the heck is that?" Bobby asked.

"Our special today is perfect for fall. A pumpkin spice crepe filled with mascarpone."

Now Bobby had to admit he hated that in the fall and the run-up to the holidays. The entire world goes pumpkin spice crazy. However, he asked for a surprise. "Oh, can I get a side of bacon, please?" Bobby knew his cholesterol was a little high, but what the heck?

"Sure, Hun, coming right up." Angie looked down. "Is that our on-call phone?" she asked.

"No," Nico said, "it's from one of his cases."

"It has a bad battery, So I have to stop by the phone store and see if I can order a new one," Bobby said.

"Don't waste your money," said Gina. "Nico, go in the back and grab that old phone. It should still be on the charger."

Bobby took the first bite of the crepe and was pleasantly surprised. It was quite tasty. Nico returned with the phone. Again, to Bobby's surprise, it was the same model, and it was vintage as the green phone. Bobby removed the back of both phones and swapped the batteries. Magically, the phone came to life. He looked at the old battery and noticed a greasy smudge on it. His old chain of evidence training kicked in.

"Nico," he said. "Can you get me a plastic bag from the back?" Nico quickly returned, and Bobby popped the old battery into the bag and the bag into his pocket. He hit enter, and the phone asked for a 4-digit code. He took out his notebook and tried Jessica's mom's birthday, MM/YY. It didn't work. He tried her dad's birthday in the same pattern. Nothing. He tried her birthday, but that wasn't it either. Setting the phone down to work on his breakfast, he wondered if the phone would lock after too many attempts. Bobby mixed the parents' months and days. No go. Modern phones now have a cloud-based backup, thought Bobby. Unfortunately, this dinosaur has no such feature.

Bobby finished his breakfast and asked Gina if he could keep the battery. She said, "Sure, Hun. In fact, keep the whole phone. Nico, get the charger for Bobby."

"Well, he didn't need to go into the phone store," Bobby concluded. The young man returned with the charger and placed it on the table. "Nico," Bobby said, "if I take the sim card out of this phone and pop it into your old phone, will it work?"

He mulled it over for a minute. "Maybe. Unless the provider has a policy against that. Either way, you may lose some contacts and information from the old phone."

"Got it," Bobby said. Bobby paid for breakfast despite his aunts' protest. Too risky, he thought. I do not want to lose anything in the transfer. Back at his office, Bobby looked at the whiteboard with all the pictures from the case. He got a magnifying glass from his desk and studied the pictures. Jessica, it seemed, was a prolific reader, and not just the books you would expect from someone her age. He referred to his notes when he first interviewed Thomas Grant. Besides ballet, filmmaking, and chess, Jessica was also something of a math prodigy. Bobby picked up the phone and tried the first four numbers of PI 3141. Not it. Damn it, he thought. I'm so close. I can feel it.

He examined the pictures again. He noticed a book next to her computer. It was by one, D. R. Kaprekar. Bobby knew nothing about advanced mathematics or Indian authors. He thought it odd reading material for a young girl, but Jessica was no ordinary child. A quick Google search revealed that Kaprekar was a famous Indian mathematician. Best known for the Kaprekar constant. The sum of which was 6174. "I don't suppose," he wondered anxiously. Bobby typed the number into the phone, and for the first time in seven years, it opened.

THIRTY:

IT'S ON

Nina had just brewed a fresh pot of coffee when she heard the buzz. It was her burner phone.

Nervously, she plucked it from her robe pocket and silenced it. She checked on Walter, who was sitting on the patio finishing his breakfast. One cup of black coffee, one hard-boiled egg, one slice of multigrain toast, and one half of a grapefruit. Walter followed his routine every morning, except on Sundays, which were reserved for brunch. A true man of discipline. The text simply read; it is time. I will text you the details within an hour. She could feel her heart racing.

"Are you alright, my love?" Walter asked from behind her.

"Oh, my god!" she exclaimed quickly, stuffing the phone back in her pocket. "Walter, you nearly gave me a heart attack!"

"I'm sorry!" Walter said, taking her in his arms. "I was getting ready to leave and wanted to get a hug and a kiss before I was on my way." They embraced, and Walter noticed a couple of things. One, Nina was extremely tense; her supple yet muscular frame was taut. Second, when he kissed her, he noticed her upper lip and forehead were damp with sweat. Walter was uncertain if she was becoming ill or anxious.

"Are you sure you are alright?" he asked. "Would you like for me to stay home with you today?"

"No!" Nina said a little too quickly. "Don't be silly. I am fine. I just need a little downtime. You are sweet to offer, though." Walter gave her one more quick hug and, as he did, he noticed something in her pocket. It felt like a phone, but he could clearly see her iPhone sitting on the kitchen island. My God, he thought, she has a second phone. Walter gathered his things and headed out the door. As he put the car into gear, he called Bobby.

"Change of plans," he said into his phone. "I have a feeling something is about to happen. How quickly can you get here?"

THIRTY-ONE:

COLLIDE

Michael awoke with a start. He overslept. What time is it? He looked at the old kitchen clock on the wall. Nine am! He leaped up and grabbed his phone; four missed calls. He opened his voice message. It was from an irate Orik Selmani.

"Where the fuck are you, you piece of shit?" The Armenian sounded furious. "You waste my time? I should put a bullet in your fucking skull!" A bead of cold sweat ran down Michael's back. He knew Selmani was not someone you wanted to piss off. He was a dangerous, cold-blooded sociopath. Michael sat down for a moment to figure out what his next move was. He felt dizzy; Feeling his heart rate rising, he could hear his heart pounding in his ears. He took two deep breaths and tried to bring his heart rate down. A wave of nausea washed over him. My God, he thought, am I having a heart attack? He ran into the little bathroom and was instantly sick. As the nausea subsided and the sweat poured down his face, he lay down on the bathroom floor. He could feel the coolness of the tile and he felt a little better. Slowly, he rose and walked to the sink, and splashed some icy water on his face. His heart rate was normalizing now, and he realized it had just been a panic attack. He brushed his teeth and rinsed his mouth to get the acrid taste out. He opened the refrigerator, got a ginger ale, and took a long sip. It did the trick, as his stomach calmed slightly. He remembered that ginger ale was his mother's favorite and... Jessica! Oh my god! He thought. He tied her up in the back of the van all night. What if she choked, screamed, or got free? He wheeled around and quickly grabbed his car keys.

A surprise knock interrupted him as he reached for the doorknob. He froze for a second. What if Selmani came to follow through with his promise to shoot him? He carefully opened the door to see a New York police officer.

"Mr. Brady?" the officer asked. For a second, Michael stood frozen. "Are you Michael Brady?" the detective repeated. Michael glanced at his car, blocked by the detective's black crown vic.

"Sorry," Michael replied. "Yes, I'm Michael Brady."

"You will need to come with me," the police officer said in a steady, non-menacing tone.

"Why? What is this all about?" Michael asked.

"There seems to be a problem at your warehouse," the detective said.

"What kind of problem?" Michael asked.

"The kind that requires your presence," the police officer said with growing agitation.

"Oh, okay, let me get my coat," Michael said. He grabbed his jacket, knowing that in the inside pocket, he had a snub nose.38, an obvious violation of his parole. His hands trembled as he put on the jacket. He returned to the door, and the detective stepped inside. He noticed the house was quite a mess.

"Is everything alright, Mr. Brady?" the officer asked. His experience told him something was off.

"I am sorry. My mother died yesterday, and now this," Michael said in a shaky voice. "I'm afraid I'm a bit of a mess at the moment." In the bedroom at the end of the hall, the detective could see a hospital bed and various prescription bottles on the nightstand.

"I'm sorry to hear that," he said. "I recently lost my father. It sucks, but you move past it." As he looked down, Michael noticed something on the floor. It was a box of tampons that he had missed. If the cop saw them, he would wonder who exactly they belonged to. He placed his hand in the jacket pocket where the gun was. He could feel the wooden grip of the gun that had belonged to his father.

"Was it just you and your mother here, Mr. Brady?" the cop asked.

"Yes, officer." Michael held his breath for a second and could tell the cop believed him. "What's happened?" Michael asked again.

"There seems to have been a break-in at your business."

Michael gasped.

THIRTY-TWO:

PHOTOGRAPH

Bobby scrolled through the pictures on Jessica's phone. He dialed Sal's number to let him know. Sal answered the phone. "Kid, you must be a mind reader. I was about to call you. Interpol information just came in. This dude is a major league asshole and all-around dangerous guy."

"In what way?" Bobby asked.

"You name it, kid. International arms dealer, drug smuggler. He did a stint as a mercenary with the Wagner group in Crimea. He has been involved in sex trafficking recently. A real malevolent fuck. Mr. Selmani's location was unknown to Interpol, who contacted the FBI. You can expect a visit soon from one of our heroes in the bureau."

Sal had a genuine contempt for the FBI. He felt they were all grand-standers who made deals with scumbags to find bigger scumbags. Often, he thought they impeded actual police work. Bobby had worked on several cases with them. He thought that while they could be a little cocky, they were professional and could bring to bear the formidable power of the federal government. He secured confessions out of at least ten perps by just hinting at federal involvement in a case. The feds had their own prisons, not to mention the death penalty. Sal's advice, kid, "stay away from the guy and let the Feds deal with him."

"What is the guy's name?" Bobby asked.

"Shit, sorry, kid. His name is Orik Selmani. How is that for a handle? Sounds like some kind of fancy toothbrush." Sal laughed.

"Got it!" Bobby said. It was only then he remembered why he had called. "Sal, I got the phone open!" Bobby exclaimed.

"What phone?" Sal asked.

"Jessica Grant's phone," Bobby replied.

"You've got to be shitting me?!" Sal exclaimed. "How the fuck—" Bobby cut him off.

"It is a long story. I want to drop it back off so your IT guys can go through it."

"Kid," Sal said. "You are one in a million! No evidence for years, then suddenly within weeks, bang! You bust in the open."

"Thanks, but I'm not sure if anything here is helpful, but it's a start," said Bobby. "I'll ask Autumn to identify anyone and get it back to you within the hour."

"I will let our tech folks know. Bobby," Sal said. "Outstanding work!"

"Thanks, Sal."

Bobby called Autumn and asked if she could meet him at Ernie's, and she happily agreed. When he arrived, she was already waiting for him at a booth. As he walked up to her, she stood up, and she rewarded him with a serious kiss and a warm embrace. For a second, Bobby forgot why he was there.

"What's happening, Bobby?" she asked, jolting him out of his affection-induced fog.

"Oh, sorry. I got the phone open," he said.

"Are you kidding?" She gasped. "What is in it? Will it be helpful? Have you spoken to Thomas or to the police?"

"Easy," Bobby said. "One thing at a time."

"Can you look at these pictures and let me know if you recognize anyone or anything?" Just then, Ernie sidled up to the booth with fresh coffee.

"And how are you two lovebirds doing this morning?" Both Autumn and Bobby blushed, but neither of them denied the sentiment.

"Bobby got Jessica's phone open!" Autumn said.

"What?!" Ernie replied. "Darla, come over here!" Darla glided over, smiling at the group.

"What is all the excitement about?" she asked.

"They found Jessica's phone and got it to open!" Ernie said.

"You're kidding!"

Bobby explained he was on his way to the police station to give it back to them. "Before I do, though, I was hoping you might identify some of these people or places." Autumn, Darla, and Ernie huddled around the phone and gazed at the photos.

"Oh, look, there is one of you, dear," Darla said, referring to Autumn. Bobby glanced at it. Just as quickly, Autumn moved to the next photo.

"I hate the way I look in pictures!" she said. "Plus, I was ten pounds lighter than I am now."

"I think you are more beautiful now," Bobby said without thinking. Autumn blushed. Ernie and Darla shared a knowing smile.

"Wait, who's that guy?" Autumn asked. "She seems to have taken a few pictures of him."

"He looks familiar," Ernie said as he examined the picture closer. "And that looks like the alley across the street, doesn't it?" All three agreed.

"Right," Darla said "Mark, no... Mike, something or other."

"Michael," Ernie corrected her. He always preferred Michael.

"That's right," Darla said. "Didn't he have some sort of business around here?"

"He had those DVD rental machines. Michael wanted to place one outside the diner, but I did not think it was a smart idea to have people congregating outside the diner when it was closed. He went out of business," Ernie said.

"I just remember him always being defeated and sad looking," Darla said. Simultaneously, Autumn and Bobby said, "The Sad Man!" Just then, Bobby's phone rang.

"Hi, Walter," Bobby said on the phone. "Damn, I'll be right there."

THIRTY-THREE

BREAK IN

E d Getz had been on his way out the door when Sal asked him to pick up the break-in. Normally, they would have sent a squad car to a simple B&E. They found a suspicious package in the subway, prompting an evacuation with all available units assisting. "Come on, Sal, I was on my way home." Getz had protested.

"It should only take an hour," Sal had assured him. "You can come in late tomorrow to even things out."

"I should just fucking retire," Getz mumbled. "What's that?" Sal asked. "I said have a good night, Captain."

As he rolled up to Michael Brady's house, he thought, What a shitty neighborhood. Looks like a good place to get mugged.

After identifying himself and speaking with Michael for five minutes, Getz thought he would speed things up by taking the guy to his warehouse. As they drove, Getz noticed that Michael Brady seemed extremely nervous. He wondered if there was more to his concern than just his business. Michael was feeling a little dizzy. He was trying to breathe evenly. Surely, if they had found Jessica, he would already be in custody. "Who the hell would break into the warehouse?" Michael wondered aloud.

"I'm not sure, Mr. Brady. That is what we are going to find out," Getz said. "Do you keep anything valuable there?" Michael shook his head. Well, he thought, unless you consider a kidnapped girl who has been missing for seven years and whom an Armenian mobster was about to give me ten grand for.

"No," Michael said, "not really."

Michael noticed the garage door wasn't closed completely. They entered the building, and the van was gone. "The van!" Michael exclaimed. "It's gone."

His mind was racing; then it occurred to him. Selmani, he thought. His goons broke in and took what they came for.

"What van?" the detective asked. "Has there been a vehicle stolen?" Michael froze for a second. Shit, he thought. I do not want the NYPD to find his van with Jessica in the back. He panicked.

"No, it's okay," Michael said, nonsensically. It was an old, beat-up van. Not a big deal.

"I will still have to file a stolen vehicle report," Getz said. "Is there anything else missing that you notice?" Getz asked as he turned around. To the detective's shock, Brady had drawn a .38 from his pocket.

"G-get on the ground!" Michael said in an unsteady voice. "Now!"

Getz said calmly, "Mr. Brady, I do not know what this is about, but trust me on this. You do not want to shoot a cop." Michael's hands were shaking as Getz slid his hand down to his Glock in a pancake holster on his waist.

"Stop!" Michael shouted without thinking. He panicked and two shots erupted from the weapon.

THIRTY-FOUR:

BANG

Bobby was hurrying to his car with Autumn. He parked in front of the diner and was kissing Autumn when shots rang out.

"Was that a firecracker?" Autumn asked, but Bobby knew all too well that it was not. The shot had come from the alley across the street.

"Autumn, go back inside the diner. Ernie will protect you and call 911 and explain that you heard two gunshots," Bobby said.

"Wait," Autumn replied.

"Autumn!" Bobby said in a deadly serious tone that she had not heard before. "Go now!" With tears streaming down her face, she ran to the diner.

Bobby opened the trunk, grabbed something, and tossed his cane in the car. He crossed the street into the alley. As he carefully rounded the corner, he drew his Browning.45 high-power. As he peered out, he saw a man who gently pulled the black crown Vic into the garage. Bobby knew immediately from the style and markings that it was a police car. Shit! Bobby thought, hold my ground or go in?

His training kicked in and he closed the distance on the open garage door. He peaked around the corner. Using the cinder block wall as a partial cover, he quietly inched his way into the structure.

Michael was in full panic mode. He had just killed a New York City detective! He hadn't meant to, but he had just the same. They would hunt him like a dog. He needed to leave town, but how? His first instinct was that of a child. Conceal the car and the dead cop until he could think. He would pull the car out of sight and then take a cab back to the house and get his mom's car. He needed her life insurance and the $10k from Orik to disappear. More than anything else, he needed time. Could he make it to Mexico before they found the cop? Does Canada have extradition? As he turned around to lower the garage door, he saw a large man with a gun pointed directly at him.

"Mister," Bobby said slowly and calmly. "Keep your hands where I can see them, get down on your knees, and interlock your finger behind your head." Michael felt his coat pocket for his gun. Then he saw it lying on the ground three feet away. He tried to protest, but Bobby cocked the hammer back on the.45 and said, "I won't tell you a second time." Michael complied, and Bobby immediately recognized him as the "Sad man" in Jessica's photos. Michael wondered if he could reach the gun before getting shot. Maybe a quick death, go out in a blaze of glory? He immediately discarded the thought. Michael was, in his heart of hearts, a coward. He knelt with his hands behind his head and wept. Bobby moved closer, kicking the gun away. He recognized the detective on the ground as Ed Getz. "Ed, holy shit." A wave of anger swept over Bobby. Sure, Getz had always given him a tough time, but they graduated from the academy together and he sure as shit did not deserve to die like this. For a brief second, Bobby thought, I should just shoot this son of a bitch, but then he thought of Jessica and Autumn and the fact that he was not that kind of guy. He had killed people during the war, and hadn't he discharged his weapon once in the line of duty as a police officer? Yes, but he was not a cold-blooded killer. From behind him, Bobby heard at least two squad cars rolled up behind him, and the officers ordered Bobby to lower his weapon. It was Bobby's turn to kneel and put his weapon on the ground. Just then, he heard Sal.

"Officers, stand down. He is one of us."

"Shit," Bobby thought. "I'm going to end up owing that Sicilian another favor."

THIRTY-FIVE

DON'T LOSE HER

"**B**obby, what the hell is going on here?" Sal asked. The officers took custody of Michael, cuffed him, and read him his Miranda rights, per regulations. Bobby and Sal immediately assessed Getz. He was breathing. He had two wounds; one bullet had grazed his temple and took off part of his left ear. It was bleeding profusely, but it was not life-threatening. The second was an upper chest wound closer to his collarbone, missing the subclavian artery by an inch. It seemed more serious, but it also looked to have been through and through. Bobby pulled a handkerchief from his pocket and applied direct pressure to the chest wound. A flood of police and EMTs arrived and quickly took over, attending to Getz's wounds. As they rolled him away, Sal turned again to Bobby.

"Kid, what the hell—" Bobby cut him off.

"I heard gunfire from across the street. Sal, I think this same asshole that shot Ed. Might be responsible for the disappearance of Jessica Grant."

"You have to be fucking kidding me!" Sal said in an uncharacteristically high-pitched voice. He filled Sal in on the pictures on Jessica's phone, which he gave back to him along with his passcode. "Bobby, you'll have to come to the station and make a statement. I'm going to go to the hospital and check on Getz," Sal said.

"Can I meet you there? There's something I need to follow up on related to the other case." Bobby replied.

"Sure, kid, but just remember that a cop got shot. I don't have to tell you what a big deal this is."

Bobby nodded. "As soon as I can, I'll get there. Oh, by the way—" Bobby pulled the other phone battery out of his pocket. "This is the original battery from her phone. It looks like it has a print on it." Sal put the phone in the same plastic bag as the battery. The lab guys had arrived, and Bobby could hear Sal shouting instructions on processing the scene as he ducked under the yellow police tape. Bobby saw the police had blocked off the alley, and a crowd of people, including reporters, had gathered. He saw Autumn and Ernie across the street. Autumn ran over to him.

"Are you alright?" she asked, her face a mask of genuine concern.

"I'm fine," Bobby said. "The guy from Jessica's picture shot a cop. I'm not sure how it's all related, but there is some place I need to be. So, I have to go now." Bobby was a bit too dismissive. He instantly regretted it, seeing the hurt on her face. "Sorry Autumn," Bobby said, embracing her. "I'm a little upset. I know the cop who was shot."

"Oh, Bobby, I'm so sorry," Autumn said. "Will he be, okay?" Bobby gave her a thin smile.

"I don't think he is likely to die," he replied. "I will call you later. It may be late. I need to give a statement at the station."

"Call me regardless of the hour, or stop by my apartment," she said.

"Thank you, I may take you up on that," Bobby said as he walked to his car. As Bobby pulled away from the curb, he hit the redial on his phone. "Walter," he said into the phone. "I am sorry I got delayed. Has Nina left yet?"

"No," Walter nervously said. "She is just getting in her car now. Are you close by?"

"No, I am 15 minutes away," Bobby replied.

"That's great," Walter said, with obvious irritation.

"It's complicated, Walter. I was involved in a shooting." There was a pause.

"What does that mean you were involved in a shooting?" Walter asked.

"It does not matter, Walter. Where are you?"

"I am parked in my car a block from his house," Walter said.

"Okay, you are going to have to follow her until I can intercept you both. Leave your speaker phone on and just tell me what direction you are traveling in and on what street," Bobby said calmly.

"I cannot do that. I am not familiar with surveillance techniques. Anyway, she will recognize his car," Walter replied.

"Walter," Bobby said, "give her at least three car lengths in between, and try to let another car in between you."

"I'm going to screw this up," Walter said. "This is what I pay you for, isn't it?"

"Just relax, it is all going to be alright. Just call out the street names as you go, and do not lose her." Walter did as he was told and, in a monotone mechanical voice, began calling out directions and street signs. Ten minutes went by, and Bobby was closing the distance.

"Oh, shit!" Walter said. "She is pulling over; what should I do?" He was panicking.

"Walter, do you have space to pull over a few car lengths back?" Bobby asked.

"No, I am almost on top of her," Walter said.

"No problem, just pull up to the next block and stop," Bobby replied. "Don't turn your head, adjust your mirror and tell me what you see." Walter adjusted his mirror and watched. A man had been waiting on a bench near Nina's car. He stood, grabbed a duffle bag, and strolled to her car. Nina rolled down her window, and the man placed the bag in the passenger seat. He said something to Nina, who nodded, and the man turned and walked the other way. Walter conveyed all he saw to Bobby.

"Is that the guy, Bobby?"

"Don't overthink it, Walter. We can unpack it all later." He could hear Walter taking deep breaths to calm himself down.

"I don't know how the hell you manage this!" he said between deep breaths. "I'm not sure I am paying you enough." Bobby was still six blocks away and coming from the opposite direction. "Oh God, here she comes," Walter said into the phone.

"Walter," Bobby said, "I need you to lean your seat back and scrunch down." Water did just as Nina drove past. Nina was so preoccupied and nervous that she never saw him. As he picked up the tail, Walter noticed a black SUV two car lengths behind him. As Nina approached the same diner, she met Orik Selmani for the first time. She suddenly pulled in and parked. Walter reacted too slowly and parked two blocks away from the diner. Nina got out of her car, walked across the street, and got in a black Chevy SUV facing the opposite direction. Desperately, Walter tried to turn around, but traffic was heavy, and he couldn't even get out of the parking space. "Shit! Bobby, I'm stuck!" He explained the situation.

"It's alright, Walter." Bobby said. "I have them in sight. I will take it from here." Walter breathed a sigh of relief.

"How did you anticipate that?" Walter asked in near disbelief.

"You did a great job. You can relax now." Bobby didn't tell the client he was lucky to be headed in the right direction. Nina, what mischief are you up to? Bobby wondered.

THIRTY-SIX:

BAG FULL OF MONEY

"What's in the bag?" Selmani inquired with a malicious smile. Nina opened the black duffle bag to display three hundred thousand dollars. The minimum price they had agreed upon to take part in the day's festivities. He barked out a command to the man seated directly behind Nina. Nina said nothing. "Phone," he said.

"What?" Nina asked.

"Give him your phone." The man in the back grabbed her purse. Nina tried to protest, but Selmani thrust a 9mm pistol into her ribcage. The man in the backseat roughly tore Nina's Coach purse open and dumped the contents onto the seat beside him.

"Bitch has two phones," he said.

"Two phones?" Selmani asked. "Why, Mrs. Adams, only naughty girls have two phones." Nina's heart was racing. She had met Nickolas Gracen of the Federal Bureau of Investigation six months earlier at an Anti-human trafficking fundraiser. She had been first struck by the man's charisma and Bond-like demeanor. Human trafficking sickened and repulsed Nina and her husband. Walter, at one point, excused himself from the conversation. A friend of his was volunteering at the event and took Walter to peruse some of the silent auction items up for bid. Nina stayed and carried on the conversation with Gracen. Over the next several months, Nina kept up the communication with him, and the two had grown close. Not in a romantic sense, but as two people who shared a common cause. She had eventually disclosed to him the reason for her passion for against the exploitation of women. She confided in him she was aware of a series of events and clubs that catered to questionable erotic pursuits. He recruited Nina, who was eager to help infiltrate and eradicate a trafficking cell. It had been Gracen that Nina had stopped for on the street. Gracen had given her the duffle of non-sequential bills and had also provided her with the burner phone with a tracing beacon embedded in it. The same device the Armenian in the back seat was now holding. He laughed and threw the burner and Nina's iPhone out the window. Just like in the movies, a random delivery truck coming in the opposite direction crushed both phones within seconds of them hitting the pavement. Nina gasped as he did so.

"Don't worry," Selmani said. "I'm sure your husband has phone insurance." He laughed. Nina was now very much on her own. Per standard procedure, the FBI had multiple pursuit teams involved in the operation. When Nina got in the car in the opposite direction, it added another level of complexity. Two cars were waiting a few blocks away as part of the pursuit teams. All of whom were facing the wrong direction. They had immediately turned around to change direction, but as Walter had experienced, the traffic was heavy.

"Shit," Gracen said. Instructing the driver to do a U-turn. At that very moment. An overly aggressive stockbroker had just finished a two-martini lunch. She then blew through the traffic light, striking Gracen's SUV broadside. She had sped up to 60 miles per hour as she went through the light. The BMW impacted the SUV on the passenger side, instantly killing Special Agent Nickolas Gracen.

THIRTY-SEVEN:

ALL ALONE

B obby saw a black SUV suddenly make a U-turn to his left after he cleared the traffic light. He sped up slightly to avoid the vehicle. "Go back to Jersey, you moron!" Bobby yelled his stock answer at the driver. He was glad he hadn't switched out cars with his father yet. Compared to his Hyundai, the Ford had a more powerful six-cylinder engine, and the Fusion was invisible. Bobby wondered where Nina was going and who she was with. He thought it could be the Armenian that Sal had warned him about. Bobby was making a call when he heard a tremendous roar behind him to his left. He looked in his rearview mirror and saw the black SUV spin and roll onto the driver's side. He also saw a severely damaged car in the middle of the road with smoke pouring out of it. "Oh my God!" Bobby exclaimed. His first instinct was to stop and give aid, but he couldn't lose Nina again. So, he did the next best thing. He called 911 to report the accident. The operator confirmed fire and the EMT were on their way. She took his name and number in case they needed to contact him. Bobby did not realize the overturned vehicle belonged to the FBI, nor did he realize it was part of a surveillance detail and that the other units were hopelessly stuck in the crash's wake. Bobby, in fact, was now the only person following Nina. The FBI immediately reached out to the NYPD for help. The latter wasn't pleased with an operation in the city without prior notice. Gracen made a note of the vehicle make, model, and license number. Unfortunately, the accident had happened so quickly that he wasn't able to forward the information to his team. Bobby was three car lengths behind Selmani's vehicle on the passenger side. From Bobby's vantage point, he couldn't see that they had placed something over Nina's head. Nina was panicking a bit, but she thought Gracen couldn't be far behind, only he wasn't. Bobby followed as Selmani neared the outskirts of the city. He turned onto Winchester Street near the old Creedmoor mental hospital, long abandoned and a truly dangerous section of the city. It was becoming increasingly hard for Bobby to follow without being detected. He turned his car on a parallel street and took out his binoculars. Bobby watched the SUV slow down and pull into a long-abandoned warehouse. He could see a dock door raise and the SUV pull in. *Shit!* Bobby thought, now what? Time to call in the cavalry. He rang Sal's line, but it went to voicemail. "Damn it Sal, pick up!"

Bobby weighed his options. Hold his ground or close in. He rang Sal's phone again, but again it went straight to voicemail. He was running out of options. If Nina was in danger, what was his best course of action? What kind of force numbers and opposition would he likely encounter? No doubt he would be outmanned and outgunned. In the end, it simply didn't matter. The Marine in Bobby took over. As far as he was concerned, it was time to move out. He left one last message for Sal, giving him his location, what he had seen, and his intent to reconnoiter the area.

THIRTY-EIGHT

THE BOX

The police sat Michael in interrogation room three, affectionately known in the station as "the box." The officers cuffed Michael's hands and attached them to an iron bar connected to the table. His head was spinning, his heart racing as he tried to think of what to do. The smartest thing to do is to ask for an attorney right away, he thought. It's estimated that 40-55% of interrogations end in a confession. Even hardened criminals can fall prey to the pressure and techniques used by modern law enforcement. While no two interrogations were the same, Michael was obviously highly uncomfortable. Sal and Detective Diana Battle watched through the two-way mirror. They turned up the heat literally in the box to make the suspect even more uncomfortable.

"Sal, how do you want to manage this?" Diana inquired. "He might ask for an attorney if he does not have a stroke."

"You go first, D, and calm him down," Sal said. "We should convey that we believe it was an accidental shooting caused by a misunderstanding."

Another detective came in and handed Sal Michael's rap sheet and the results from Jessica's phone dump. The cell battery's fingerprints matched Michael's, as Bobby had predicted.

"Holy Shit!" Sal said. "Not only did this asshole shoot Getz, but he also had something to do with Jessica Grant's disappearance!" Battle's eyes went wide with that news.

"You're kidding!" Diana said.

"Hold up, D, let this piece of crap sweat for a while. Let's check something out." Sal went back to his office to reach out to Bobby for more info on the phone. He noticed Bobby had called his cell four times. Sal hit the redial button, and Bobbie immediately picked up. "Kid, you will not believe this—" Before Sal could finish, Bobby interrupted.

"Sal, they took her to an abandoned warehouse off of Winchester near the old mental hospital!"

"What? They who?" Sal asked. "What are you talking about?"

"Nina Adams," Bobby said. "I think that Orik Selmani character has my client's wife in an abandoned building." Bobby recounted his tale of Nina and Selmani, the black SUV that had been T-boned, and his current predicament at the location. Before Sal could respond, his office door swung open, and in walked the Chief of Police flanked by what could only be the FBI with their sunglasses and dark suits.

"Sal," the Chief said, "We have a situation."

Jesus, help me! Sal thought. How soon can I retire?

"Kid, hang tight." Then Bobby's phone went dead.

"No... wait Fuck!" Bobby tried not to cuss, but some situations called for just one word.

THIRTY-NINE:

SODOM AND GAMMORRAH

Nina was breathing deeply beneath the hood. "Excuse me," she said, "I would like to take off this hood. I am a little claustrophobic, and it's freaking me out!"

"No," a voice answered coarsely. "Keep it on and shut your mouth." Nina was trying her best not to hyperventilate. Over the past twenty minutes, they had headed east, from what she could tell. She tried to focus in on the feeling and sounds, to distract her from claustrophobia and orient her to their destination. She thought they had gone through a tunnel; if so, that would have been the midtown tunnel. She estimated they had been driving for twenty or thirty minutes. If accurate, they would be in Queens.

"Relax," said Selmani, "We are almost there." Gracen had told her to play along when she arrived, pick whatever girl they showed her. Once Nina was out of harm's way, Gracen's FBI team would swarm the building. A second team, along with local police, would surround and stop the vehicle Nina was in. An overwhelming show of force would guarantee her safety, along with the girl she had brought out with her. The plan seemed solid, but Nina had no point of reference, just what she had seen on television and in the movies. The SUV made several turns and then stopped. It beeped the horn twice and she could hear a heavy door slide open. The car moved forward, and the door closed as the SUV stopped, all of which Nina noted. Someone removed Nina's hood. Her eyes took a second to adapt to the light. She could smell a dank odor. Stepping out of the SUV, a man with an excess of cologne seized her arm.

"This way," he said, attempting charm. "We have quite a variety of merchandise. We are confident we can find what you are looking for."

Merchandise? Nina thought. How can this son of a bitch think of these poor women as merchandise? Nina could see that this had once been a ware-house of some sort. There were half a dozen armed men milling about with assault style rifles, others with pistols. Nina knew little about guns. Walter gave Nina a pistol and insisted she learn to shoot, but that was the extent of her fire-arm knowledge. Selmani opened a door for Nina, and as she walked through, her mouth dropped open. Inside was a fully remodeled space featuring soaring ceilings. She saw they had plastered and painted the walls. A mahogany, fully stocked bar stood on one side of the room. Perhaps twenty-five people had gathered near the bar. All of them were drinking and chatting.

"What the hell is this?" Nina asked.

"You didn't think you would be the only one bidding in our auction." Selmani laughed.

Auction. Who the fuck does this pig think he is? Nina's fear was slowly being replaced by rage and contempt. This wasn't some chichi little auction at Sotheby's or Christie's. These were human beings! This was modern-day slav-ery. These perverts were all going down! Nina only hoped that she would get the satisfaction of testifying in court. She would point her finger at Selmani and say, "yes, this piece of shit is the guilty party." Nina scanned the room and was disgusted to see that some of these people were in the same circles as her and Walter. Black tie events, gold-plated fundraisers, hypocrites one and all. The bile rose in Nina's throat. She inquired about a nearby restroom. Selmani pointed her toward the lady's room and motioned for one of his men to escort her.

FORTY:

SNAFU

Sal listened as the FBI special agent in charge, Woodrow Allen, laid out what had gone wrong. During an operation, the lead agent died in a traffic accident while following the suspect.

"Died where?" Sal asked.

"The accident took place on East 36th. The pursuit vehicle was struck and rolled on its side. It killed both agents instantly," the Fed said.

"The vehicle was T-boned," Sal said, beginning to put the pieces together.

"What?" Allen asked.

"Sorry, hang on a minute." Sal picked up his phone, but Bobby had hung up, or the connection had dropped. As he dialed the number, Sal asked Agent Allen the name of the informant that they had been following. Agent Allen mechanically replied, "I cannot disclose the name of the informant as the information is classified." "Damn!" Sal exclaimed. "You're running an op in our city, you fucked it up, and now you won't give me the name of who you want me to help you find?!"

Bobby picked up. "Sal, what the hell?" Bobby whispered. "Where did you go?"

"Sorry, kid, all hell is breaking loose here. What's the name of your client?" Sal asked.

"Her name is Nina Adams, and she is in deep shit!" Bobby replied.

"Hang on, Bobby. Is your informant's name Nina Adams?" Sal asked Allen.

Bewildered, the agent said, "How the fuck do you know that?" Sal ignored him.

"Kid, give me your address; I'm sending a bunch of cops your way." Bobby gave him the approximate address. "Bobby, stay put and hold your position," Sal said and ended the call. Immediately, Bobby received a text from an app allowing Sal to track Bobby's phone. Bobby didn't realize there was such a thing, but he instantly agreed. Bobby realized they would take at least twenty minutes to get there. His intuition told him he didn't have that much time. He cautiously made his way toward the warehouse. If these animals were as cautious as he thought, they would have security cameras. Bobby used binoculars to discover cameras at each corner of the building's front. Damn, Bobby thought. He moved to the eastern side of the building once again, camera. As he moved to the western edge of the building, he saw no camera, so he crept closer. His leg was aching, but there was no time for that now. He saw they boarded the windows up on the western side. There was no door or access except for one tiny window on the ground level. Slowly, Bobby made his way in that direction.

FORTY-ONE

BIDDING

When Nina was alone in the restroom, she tried to regain her composure. She rinsed her mouth out to get rid of the acrid bile taste. She splashed cold water on her face and looked at herself in the mirror. "You can do this!" she affirmed to her image. "You must! She took a deep breath before leaving the mirror and heading to the door. She noticed a tiny window just above the toilet. Nina wondered, Could I fit through that? She immediately dismissed the thought. Even though she worked out religiously and was careful with what she ate, there was no way in hell her hips would slip through that space. She opened the door to find one of Selmani's henchmen waiting for her. As she exited, she excused herself as she passed another woman. Da-Xia Wong. Wong had met Nina at several fundraisers over the years. She and her husband, Liang, owned several businesses in Chinatown. One was a highly regarded restaurant. To all outward appearances, a real Horatio Alger tale of success. The restaurant was, however, a front for their actual business, prostitution. They catered to wealthy Chinese men visiting New York on business and on the prowl for young, sometimes very young, American girls. Wong was there to replenish her stable. When a girl reached a certain age, or lost that childlike look. Wong would sell them to a trafficker who specialized in the human organ market. She immediately recognized Nina and remembered that she had tried to invite her to an anti-trafficking event. She went directly to the guard and said, "I need to speak to Orik Selmani immediately."

Nina accepted the champagne and sipped it to steady her nerves. They gave her a numbered paddle and took her seat. They ushered the first woman into the center stage. The bidding began and quickly escalated to $50,000. "Going once, twice... Sold," the auctioneer said matter-of-factly. Nina made a mental note of the monster that had bought the little girl. She regretted not having her phone to document the proceedings. She looked at her watch and wondered when the Feds would burst in. What were they waiting for? Several more transactions took place, and Nina got nervous. What if something has gone wrong? She remembered Gracen had told her if all else failed, make a purchase and don't raise any suspicion, the FBI would intercept them as they left the building. Nina noticed a young girl being ushered to the center of the makeshift stage. She was young, blonde, and terrified. Nina estimated she was only about fifteen. My God, Nina thought. They had dressed her in a very short, gold lame dress. A wave of nausea struck Nina. She took a deep breath and fought back the feeling. The bidding had begun, and she was receiving a lot of attention. Bidding was up to $60,000. The Asian man smiled as the auctioneer said, "Going once, going twice—" but before he could finish, Nina raised her paddle.

"Sixty-five thousand," Nina said. The man shot her an angry stare.

"Seventy thousand," he said confidently.

"One hundred and fifty thousand," Nina said. The man crossed his arms in disgust.

"Going once, twice... Sold." Nina felt both relief and utter disgust. She had just purchased another human being. No matter what her intention, the transaction disturbed her to her very core. Another two auctions occurred, and the Auctioneer said, "Ladies and gentlemen, we will take a brief break while we replenish our merchandise. Please, head over to our refreshment area. If you have already finished bidding, you can collect your purchases shortly." Nina committed every detail of the man's face to memory. Someday soon, she thought, I will see you again. Behind bars.

"Madam, please follow me," a man said pleasantly. Nina complied.

Da-Xia Wong was furious. When Selmani entered the office, she erupted.

"You insolent dog. How dare you keep me waiting?" No one spoke to Selmani in this manner.

"I'm not sure I heard you correctly," he said. She immediately realized she had made a potentially fatal mistake.

"My apologies," she said suddenly, showing submission, bowing, and diverting her gaze. Selmani regained his composure and smiled.

"Madam Wong, what can I do for you?"

"The tall white woman," she said tentatively.

"What about her?" Selmani asked.

"She isn't who you think she is."

"Bring me her bag," he said. "Who is it you think she is?" he laughed. As Selmani looked in the bag, he noticed all the money was still there. "Have we settled the account yet?" he asked.

"No, she just received her purchase," the accountant responded.

"Did you check this bag for bugs and trackers?" Selmani asked, a slight concern creeping into his voice.

"Of course," the accountant assured him. Selmani opened the bag. Wong drew closer to peek as well. Selmani took the money out and stacked it. As he slammed the third stack of hundred-dollar bills onto the table, a dye pack inserted into the bills exploded. It covered the bills but also Selmani and Dai-Xia's faces. Both lurched back and immediately wiped their faces. They used the dye pack to taint money taken in bank robberies. The pack appeared identical in weight and appearance to the others. However, it contained a small incendiary device in a hollowed-out cavity and effectively covered both the currency and the robbers with permanent ink. They used money taken from a bank robbery that had been in evidence for several years, but the FBI missed removing the dye pack. Selmani screamed in anger. He ran to a mirror. The blue/green ink appeared in dots and splotches on the left side of his face. Madam Wong took an even heavier spray, as she didn't move as quickly.

"Bring me that bitch. Now!" Selmani screamed.

FORTY-TWO:

LAST STAND

Nina approached the girl who she had just purchased/liberated. "Hello, my name is Nina, and don't worry. I'll get you out of here. What's your name?" The girl hesitated at first, but Nina reassured her. "It's alright." The little girl looked around.

"My name is Jessica," she said, just above a whisper. "Jessica Grant." Nina nodded her head and then it hit her. Holy shit, Nina thought. Before Nina could ask where they had held her for so long, a commotion from the office caught her attention. Two of Selmani's men were running over toward them. Nina grabbed Jessica by the hand and ran towards the bathroom. Suddenly, the Auctioneer jumped in front of them, his arms and legs spread wide like he was a defender in a basketball game. Nina, surging with adrenaline, remembered the "target-focused training" she had taken years before. She brought her forearm up the man's throat. Causing him to gasp, she had struck his windpipe. Both of his hands reflexively went to his throat. Then Nina drove her foot into his groin area like she was punting a football. He fell like a sack of potatoes to the ground. Nina and Jessica made it to the bathroom door first, and once inside, Nina locked it. Now what? she thought.

"Where are you, Gracen?" she said aloud, not knowing he was on a slab in the morgue across town. "The window," she told Jessica, who was crying. The men were kicking at the door. Nina, ever resourceful, noticed a chair, grabbed it, and slid it under the doorknob. She saw that the door also had one of those automatic closing devices, no doubt left over when the building was a factory. She climbed on a chair and took off her belt, wrapping it around both arms of the device. "Let's go," she urged Jessica, making her way to the little window. Nina opened the small casement window. She jumped back when she noticed a large man outside the window.

"Nina, I'm here to get you out," Bobby said. "Walter sent me!" Now her head was spinning.

"Walter?" she asked.

"There is no time to explain," Bobby replied.

"This is Jessica," Nina stated.

"Jessica Grant?!?" Bobby said in utter shock.

"Take her first." Jessica climbed onto the back of the toilet, and Bobby helped her up to the window. Jessica strained to force herself through the window. Bobby pulled, Nina pushed, and like a cork from a bottle, Jessica popped out of the window.

"You're next," Bobby said. Nina scrambled up onto the toilet, but try as they might, Nina could not fit through the space.

"It's no use. Get her out of here," Nina pleaded.

"Not without you!" Bobby said. Outside, the men shot at the splintered door and kicked it harder.

"Go!" Nina begged just as the door frame failed.

"Nina, lay flat on the ground!" Bobby said. He aimed his Browning High Power just as a man burst through the door. "Police, drop your weapon!" he yelled. It startled the man at first, but he raised his Uzi, anyway. Bobby fired two shots from the .45. Both shots hit the center mass, just as they had trained him to do both in the Marines and at the police academy. The man flew back and out of the door. A second man tried to enter again. Bobby shot two more volleys, and the second man also fell to the ground. An Armenian appeared from the side of the building, flanking Bobby.

Huddled on the ground next to Bobby, Jessica screamed, "Look out!" The man brought his gun around and aimed at Jessica. In sheer desperation, Bobby somehow leaped to his feet to cover her with his body as he raised his gun. Both rounds struck Bobby in the chest, and he slumped back against the wall. Jessica screamed. The man took aim once more, this time at Bobby's head. Suddenly, a shot rang out, and the Armenian fell forward onto the ground, dead. Bobby looked up just as Diane Battle rounded the corner.

"I have one offender and one civilian down. I need a bus at his location, forthwith!" Diane screamed into her tactical radio. Diane checked the pulse of the Armenian. Dead. Bobby felt like he was sinking. He heard Jessica crying and the best sound of all, the sweet sirens of the combined forces of the NYPD, FBI, and HRT teams. Bobby was struggling to breathe, and pain radiated from his chest.

"Bobby," Diane said. "Stay with me." She laid him down on his back.

"This is Jessica," Bobby said, his breath short and wispy. "My client Nina is in the bathroom."

"We are all over it, Bobby," Diane said calmly. "Stay with me." He felt very sleepy.

"Need to close my eyes," he said.

"Nope," Battle replied. "Not an option. Where is that bus?" Diane yelled into her radio.

FORTY-THREE:

CAUGHT

The NYPD and FBI swarmed the building. The Armenians, seeing the massive firepower arrayed against them, quickly gave up the fight and laid down their weapons. A pack of Feds quickly collected Nina, along with Jessica in a Bureau Suburban, and whisked them away to the precinct. The dye pack's permanent ink decorated Madame Wong's face. They took custody of her along with the other pedophiles, traffickers, and profiteers. Only two people evaded the dragnet. Selmani and his driver slipped away through a tunnel under the office during the chaos. The filing cabinet concealed a trap door. They issued a Bolo for Selmani, but he evaded capture.

Michael had been waiting for several hours in the "box." He was getting agitated. When Sal and Diane Battle entered the room, he was about to ask for a lawyer, but Sal spoke first.

"Michael Brady," Sal said. "You have been a very busy boy. Let's start with shooting a New York City police officer. You know, Mr. Brady, back in the day, that alone would guarantee a trip to the morgue. Wouldn't you agree, Detective Battle?"

"Well," Diane said. "Accidents did and occasionally do still occur." Michael's heart was pounding so hard he could hear it in his ears.

"I didn't mean for that to happen!" Michael said.

"You accidentally pulled out an unregistered .38 caliber revolver, one that puts you in violation of your parole, and shot Detective Getz?" Diane asked.

"Well..." Michael replied. Before he could finish, Sal interrupted.

"Let's table that for now. Instead, let's talk about the human trafficking, kidnapping, and wrongful imprisonment of a young girl."

Beads of sweat were rolling down Michael's face. "I... I don't know what you are talking about," Michael stammered.

"No?" Sal asked. "This girl." He held the flier of Jessica, made by her father, and plastered all over Manhattan. For seven years, this copy hung on Sal's office corkboard.

"Never seen her before in my life," Michael said.

"This is her phone," Sal said, and Diane laid it on the table in front of him. "Ever seen this phone before?" Sal asked.

"N... nope," Michael said.

"Funny thing is, we found your fingerprints on it."

"Impossible," Michael said. He remembered wiping the phone before disposing of it.

"You probably think you wiped it down, but you forgot the battery," Sal said as he placed the evidence pouch with the battery in it down. It was all unraveling now. Diane excused herself from the room for a minute.

"How would you know whose phone that is?" Michael asked halfheartedly. The detective reentered the room, and Sal nodded.

"She told me." The door opened, and Jessica walked in, flanked by Diane Battle. Diane put her hand on Jessica's shoulder and whispered. "You're safe Jessica. This piece of shit will never harm you again!"

Jessica spoke clearly and firmly, saying, "That's him. He's the man who kidnapped, beat, and imprisoned me for years." She glared at Michael.

"Thank you," Sal said. Jessica paused for one more second, defiantly looking at her captor. He couldn't hold her gaze.

"I... I want a lawyer," Michael said, visibly shaken. Sal drew mere inches from his face.

"You're going to need one, you scumbag," Sal said, barely concealing his contempt. He had never felt such a powerful urge to punch someone. "We'll make sure they appoint the dumbest public defender we can find. Then we will charge you with attempted murder of a police officer, kidnapping, and human trafficking. Did you know two federal agents died today in the line of duty? They were working with us on this case," Sal said. "Detective Battle, New York state doesn't have the death penalty, does it?"

"No, Captain, it does not, but the Feds do!" she said. "Even if they don't go for that. The federal prisons that make Rikers seem like a vacation at Club Med."

"Do the murderers and rapists think highly of pedophiles in prison, Detective Battle?"

"No sir, they do not!" she replied. Her hard, cold stare bore into Michael.

"Stop! Stop!" Michael said, crying. "Please. What do you want?" Michael cradled his head in his hands and sobbed.

"Tell us where this man is." Sal said as he slid a picture of Selmani to Michael. Michael denied knowing the man. "Don't play with me, Michael!" Sal yelled.

"I swear, I've never seen him before," Michael replied.

"Okay, how about him?" Sal slid a mugshot of Valon Koci across the table. It was obvious from his reaction that Michael knew Koci.

"What kind of deal is on the table if I share what I know about this man?" Michael asked.

"It depends on the information," Detective Battle said. "How about where he keeps his stable of women?"

FORTY-FOUR

FORTRESS

The building appeared abandoned and dilapidated from the outside. It had been a hotel, then an elder care facility, and finally abandoned. Valon Koci purchased the building five years earlier through a dummy company. He had even applied for and received city redevelopment money to renovate the inside. No city official thought to follow up on the official use of the building, nor had anyone inspected it beyond its last official updates. Koci had made sure of that by handsomely paying off the local inspectors. On the bottom floor, they allowed local politicians to advertise and have rent free office space when they were running for reelection. The building looked vacant, but looks can be deceiving. They transformed the second and third floors into a very high-end brothel, catering to men of all ages and nationalities who favored the company of women, young women. The clientele comprised Wall Street insiders, politicians, and foreign nationals. The one thing they all had in common was a shared sickness and perversions for young and underage girls and, sometimes, boys. They kept the women in their rooms under lock and key on the fourth floor in less-than-ideal conditions.

Koci's opulent offices occupied the entire top floor. He spied on and covertly recorded his clients for his own protection and leverage. He had multiple income streams. His journey had begun in Los Angeles, shortly after he arrived in the US at age fifteen. Like so many before them, the Armenians banded together for protection from the more established residents, the Mexican Mafia, MS-13, and many others. Koci's initial ventures were more smash and grab operations. He gradually moved on to white-collar crimes like installing card skimmers in stores and gas stations. They would then create fake credit cards and sell them, much more lucrative and less dangerous. However, the trafficking of women and girls was by far the most lucrative part of his businesses. They would wholesale the women that were too old and didn't fit his criterion for the brothel. He also had an entire division that concentrated on the exploitation of undocumented workers seeking work in the city. His profits were astronomical. That rivaled, and most times, exceeded, any hedge fund manager or CEO in the city. He had expanded his operations to the east coast a decade ago when Selmani arrived with the news of the raid. He confirmed the total loss of the operation at the warehouse. Koci's reaction was subdued. He was irritated, but Koci had insulated himself from that aspect of the business. It would be next to impossible for them to follow the trail back to Koci. He also had all those powerful clients caught in compromising positions to use if needed. Selmani had failed him. He needed to be eliminated, but not immediately.

"Brother," he said to Selmani. "You worry too much. Sit and have a drink and calm your nerves." Koci opened a bottle of Ararat, an Armenian brandy. "A taste from the old country." He poured Selmani a snifter full. "From the waters of our homeland. Do you know they age it for years in casks that are centuries old?" he asked almost congenially.

"No," Selmani replied, taking a long bolt of the strong amber liquid. It burned the back of his throat. Selmani let out a long breath. "Valon, I do not know what happened," Selmani said, knowing full well that he hadn't done his due diligence with Nina. He had become arrogant and sloppy and missed a red flag somewhere. But that bitch will pay, he vowed to himself.

"What's on your face?" Koci asked. Noticing the ink from the dye pack. Selmani explained the situation, and fear gripped Valon Koci. "Feds," he said. "Tell me more about this woman."

FORTY-FIVE:

I KNOW A GUY

ichael's public defender had shown, and after conferring with her client and the assistant district attorney, she advised Michel to accept the terms as laid out. Michael would cooperate with the authorities, give them the address of Valon Koci's operation and turn the State's evidence against the Armenians. They lowered the most serious charge of attempted murder to reckless conduct with a firearm. They would charge him with possessing a firearm, which violated his parole. Each felony had a maximum prison sentence of five years. A far better deal than the thirty years the former sentence could and probably would have fetched. Time was of the essence, so trafficking and kidnapping charges were tabled for the time being.

Selmani and Koci were flight risks. They believed Koci had an extensive network of operations in the US, Mexico, and Canada. If he wasn't already on the run, he soon might be. Michael said he'd have to take them to Koci's building. He was absolutely terrified that Koci's men would see him and kill him on sight. The FBI assured him he would be safe, and they would factor his cooperation into federal charges forthcoming. Either way, he had little or no leverage. This was his only option. They assembled the combined task within an hour and went to Hunt's Point, once considered one of the Bronx's most dangerous areas. Neither the FBI nor the NYPD was surprised that one of these crumbling buildings was a converted, upscale brothel, nor that a ring of human traffickers would set up shop there. Michael had been there three times, once for a sort of job interview. The other two times, he had brought two young girls, both runaways, and both had unfortunately taken a ride from Michael, who had drugged them and sold them.

Michael pointed out the building to the agents responsible for his protection.

"You're sure?" Special Agent in Charge Robert Meeks asked.

"Positive," Michael said. The team called in the address, and a Federal Judge immediately granted the FBI search warrants. "Can we get out of here now?" Michael asked nervously.

"Sit back and relax," Meeks replied. "The fun starts in about fifteen minutes." The FBI ran the playbook for the combined operations once they issued the warrants. They pulled the latest floor plans for the building, and two separate teams entered the building. The FBI's elite Hostage Rescue Team, HRT for short, would lead the operations backed by an additional NYPD contingent and SWAT. Upon breaching the building, the NYPD would establish a four-block perimeter, preventing access in and out. At exactly 6:25 pm, all units were in place and ready to execute. The Federal team prepared to deploy their Stingray device. This tool allows federal technicians to disrupt cell service within a small radius. At 6:30, all teams had confirmed they were ready and in position. The Con Edison representative plunged Valon Koci's building into utter darkness. Normally, Valon had three of his thugs stationed on the street as lookouts. The police quickly took all three into custody, and with no cell service, to warn him. It caught the Armenians completely off guard as the teams gave the execution order. HRT breached the doors at the front and back of the building with small explosive charges. The guards at both doors were quickly overwhelmed. The teams deployed flash-bang grenades and swarmed into the building like angry hornets. Valon and Selmani sat frozen on the top floor for a moment, as the explosions echoed throughout the building.

"You fool," Koci said. "You have led the cops straight to me!"

"No!" Selmani replied. Before he could get another word out, Koci produced a 9mm Glock and shot Selmani in the forehead. Koci briefly considered placing Selmani's gun in his hand to claim self-defense. He was on the brink of facing a tidal wave of charges. What was one murder? Koci took a long drag on his cigar and one last sip of his cognac. The puppet master still had cards to play. He had all those powerful people caught in compromising positions to trade. Koci still had some leverage. He placed the gun on the floor. HRT violently knocked the door to his inner sanctum down, and half a dozen men in full tactical gear rushed in. Koci raised his hands above his head. This is how it ends, he thought. Not with a bang, but a whimper.

FORTY-SIX

PAPERWORK

Sal was sitting in his office organizing the literal mountain of paperwork. Shit, he thought. I'll be here all night. I think I'll need a gallon of coffee. There was a knock on his door. "Enter," Sal said irritably. The door opened, and in walked Bobby. "Kid," Sal said. "What the hell are you doing here? Shouldn't you be in the hospital?"

Bobby smiled. "I knew you would need my statement. Looking at the enormous pile of paper on Sal's desk. I don't envy you, the shit storm of paperwork this whole thing is going to bring!"

Sal grunted and chuckled. "Bobby, you don't fucking disappoint, do you? Solved a seven-year-old kidnapping case, brought down a sex trafficking ring, and saved the wife of a prominent New York financier, who also manages the NYPD's pension!"

"All in a day's work." Bobby laughed and winced with pain. When Bobby first heard the gunshots across the street from the diner, he donned his Kevlar vest. The vest had stopped the first bullet entirely, the second round made it partially through, but the tip of the bullet struck Bobby's St. Christopher's medal. It left Bobby with two enormous bruises on his chest and a sprained left arm from a fall on the pavement, which required him to wear a sling.

"Jesus, kid, talk about divine intervention," Sal said with a laugh.

"About the two men I shot," Bobby said.

"We'll get to that, kid. Mrs. Adams and Jessica both gave statements saying your actions were justified and 'overtly heroic,' to quote Mrs. Adams." Sal smiled. "When I spoke to Mrs. Adams, she said you had identified yourself as a police officer before you shot the men," Sal said with a raised eyebrow. "I reminded her you were a retired policeman. She immediately recanted what she thought she heard.

Bobby looked at the floor. "It was instinctive," he said.

"Bobby don't worry. No one is going to jam you up about that. I won't allow it."

Diane Battle knocked and entered the office. "Chief, they are here," she said. Bobby got to his feet.

"Detective, thank you for saving his life."

She smiled, looking up at Bobby. Her almost petite, five-foot three-inch frame belied the fierce tiger of the person she was. "My pleasure, Bobby," she said, shaking his hand.

Sal got up from the desk and reassured Bobby, "We take care of our own," with a slap on the back. Bobby winced. "Shit, sorry, kid, but I am glad you are here for this. Come with me." Sal ushered Bobby into the small conference room. A female officer and a counselor sat with Jessica at the table's end. She leaped to her feet when Bobby entered the room and ran to him. She threw her arms around him and hugged him. His bruised chest and sprained arm protested, but Bobby only smiled despite the pain.

Bobby heard Thomas Grant ask, "Could you tell me what this is about?" as the door opened. Thomas stepped inside. He first saw Bobby hugging someone.

"Mr. Bocchini," he said. Jessica lifted her head at the sound of her father's voice.

"Daddy!!" she said softly at first.

"Jessica?" Thomas replied. "Jessica, is that really you?" For the first time in seven years, he hugged his daughter. "How? When?" he asked. They clung to each other, weeping.

"Let's give them a few minutes," Sal managed as everyone exited the room. There wasn't a dry eye among them.

As Bobby passed, Thomas grabbed his arm. "Mr. Bocchini..."

Bobby, trying not to blubber like a baby, could only nod and pat Grant on the shoulder. Bobby walked back to Sal's office, trying his best to regain his composure. Even Sal, the original tough SOB from the Bronx, had to wipe away tears.

"This is the greatest job in the freaking world," Sal said. "On rare days like today, kid."

FORTY-SEVEN:

GREATER GOOD

Nina and Walter Adams were sitting and talking down the hall in another room. She had made her statement about Bobby's shooting at the warehouse after the FBI debriefed her.

"Nina?" Walter said. "How could you put yourself in harm's way like this? They could have killed you! Why on earth didn't you tell me?" Walter was shaking from a combination of anger, fear, and relief. He let out a long breath as he tried to calm himself down. He had spent the last several hours in panic and utter helplessness until an agent had picked him up at his home and escorted him to the station. Walter's wife was unharmed, but the details made him feel lightheaded.

"I had to do this," Nina told Walter. "Sorry that I didn't tell you. I wanted to, but you would have never approved of me taking part in this." She tilted her head to stop the flow of tears streaming down her face.

"You're damn right," he said, his face hardening. "You were being absolutely reckless!"

Nina wept. "The question is, Walter, can you forgive me? It never occurred to me what you might go through. I didn't consider the toll or impact on our relationship. I'm sorry. Please forgive me?" Nina was leaning forward, her hands resting on Walter's shoulders. Walter stood and paced the room. He desperately wanted to be mad at her. He wanted to scream at her, but it occurred to him, she hadn't been unfaithful; she had always been a champion of the downtrodden the entire time he knew her.

"That depends," Walter said, his back still to her.

"On what?" she asked. "On your promise, no, your oath, that you will do nothing like this ever again." He began to say something about the breach of trust, but the hypocrisy of that thought stung him. Had he not hired a private investigator to follow her? No, he thought. A bridge too far.

"Yes!" Nina said. "I promise I will never put myself in danger like this again. You have my word on it."

Walter turned, the couple embraced, and the incredible tension that had filled the room seemed to evaporate.

"Walter," Nina said.

"Yes, my love?" he replied.

"I have just one question."

"And what's that?" He wiped her tears with his handkerchief.

"Who is Mr. Bocchini?" she asked. Suddenly, a wave of dread swept over Walter. Now he would have to tell her he had lost faith in her and that he had hired a private detective to follow her to prove her infidelity. There was a knock on the door. The door opened, and Bobby walked in along with Sal.

"I hope I'm not interrupting anything," Bobby said. "No, Mr. Bocchini," Walter said. "It's because of you I have her safely back in his arms. In fact, Nina wondered how we became acquainted."

Bobby could plainly read the tension on Walter's face. His parents always taught Bobby to be honest, brutally honest. His mother and the nuns and priests who made up his formal education pounded that into him.

However, something told him that the truth in this instance would do more harm than good. He could always confess this later and receive absolution from Father Cavanaugh. "Your husband was worried and unaware of the situation. He asked me to follow you and, by any means necessary, keep you safe. Walter's devotion to your physical well-being and safety led me to that warehouse, Mrs. Adams, and I am glad I could do just that."

Nina smiled and buried her face in her husband's chest. Walter smiled and mouthed the words "Thank you" and winked. Bobby shot him a wink and a nod of his head. Nina cleared her throat and, noticing for the first time Bobby's sling and the bruising that was now spread to just below his neck.

"How are you Mr. Bocchini?"

"Call me Bobby," he said warmly. "Thank God for Kevlar!" Walter and Nina drew near him.

"Bobby," Walter said. "Seriously, you have performed far above my expectations. Is there anything, anything at all, we can do for you?"

A thought occurred to Bobby. He smiled, "You know, I think there is something, Walter."

FORTY-EIGHT:

PRESSER

In a hastily arranged press conference at One Police Plaza, the public affairs officer announced that a joint operation between the FBI and the NYPD had conducted a series of raids. The result of which was the complete dismantling of a major human trafficking ring. She further stated that the authorities had taken Valon Koci, the ring's leader, into custody. The authorities made at least two dozen other arrests in connection with the operation. She failed to mention some prominent names taken into custody between the warehouse and the brothel. She then introduced Special Agent Robert Meeks. He reviewed the operation details and thanked the NYPD for their help in a successful conclusion. Then it was Sal's turn to speak.

"We would like to announce we have found Jessica Grant. You may remember the little girl that went missing seven years ago. She is alive. We have reunited her with her family."

The room erupted with this bombshell as they leaped to their feet with follow-up questions. Sal silenced them. "I would also like to acknowledge retired NYPD Detective Robert Boschini for his help in this case. Mr. Bocchini was working with us as a cold case consultant. He found and developed evidence that directly led to the break in both cases." Sal's statement deviated from the script, upsetting the department and the FBI. There would be hell to pay in the days to come from his supervisors, but he didn't give a damn. He wouldn't let the Feds or NYPD take the spotlight from Bobby. Anyway, Sal thought, I've got thirty years as of January. I can pull his pin and retire any time I want.

A young female reporter from a local TV raised her hand. "When can we speak to Jessica?!"

"The family asked for time to celebrate her rescue and reconnect," Sal informed. "I'm sure that you will both understand and accommodate them at this request."

The room was bustling with energy and inquiries as Sal handed the podium back to the Public Affairs Officer with a wry smile. She glared as she strode back to the podium. The news broke like a tsunami as teams from all the major networks and national and local news organizations descended on police headquarters like a swarm of locusts.

FORTY-NINE:

CELEBRATE

The weeks that followed were hectic for most everyone involved in the cases. Newscasters and paparazzi were obsessed with trying to catch a glimpse of Jessica and her father. Everyone talked about the case. Newspapers, TV shows, true crime podcasts and social media were replete with story after story and post after post. As for Bobby, he had to change his cell number because it literally would not stop ringing. Just as he had imagined, they verbally dressed Sal down for the additions he made to the press conference, but he did not care. He was certain he did the right thing. In the end, the mayor himself spoke to the PC at the behest of his good friend and campaign contributor, Walter Adams. Grudgingly, the authorities relented and gave him his due, even adding a commendation to Sal's record for helping to solve one of the biggest missing person cases in NYPD history.

Nina and Walter remained insulated from the whirlwind of coverage, as they withheld her identity before the trial as a safety precaution. The couple enjoyed each other's company on a week-long vacation in Saint Thomas. They planned a very private celebration for Jessica and her father at the Little Italy club. Bobby and his entire family were there.

Bobby introduced Autumn to the Bocchini clan. Autumn was absolutely elated to meet his family and that her personal nightmare regarding the kidnapping was finally over.

"Bobby," his mother said. "She is a lovely girl!"

Aunt Gina said, "She's too skinny; we have to plump her up a bit."

"I think she is perfect!" Bobby said as he watched her from across the room.

"This is some shindig kid," Sal said as he clapped Bobby on the Back. "When does the guest of honor arrive?"

"Should be any minute," Bobby said.

"Bocchini. Sorry, Bobby," Ed Getz said from behind him.

"Hi Ed, how are you feeling?" Getz looked at his shoes.

"Better." The bullets didn't hit anything vital, and his recovery was moving along nicely. "I just wanted to thank you for saving his life."

"You're welcome, Ed," Bobby said. "But really, you don't have to thank me. I was just protecting a brother in blue. I know that if the situation had been reversed, you would have done the same thing for me."

"Yeah," Getz said, now smiling. "Only I would've gotten there before they shot you. You know, cause you're such a lard ass." Both men laughed.

"Jesus, Getz," Sal said, laughing too.

"Eddy," Bobby's mom said, joining the conversation. "You're looking better." She had sent several days of meals to him when he arrived home from the hospital. "Don't forget our Saturday breakfast gatherings now that you are feeling better."

Just then, Walter and Nina walked in. Bobby and Sal excused themselves and walked over to greet them. They appeared deeply in love and very tanned.

"How were the islands?" Sal asked.

"Like heaven," Nina said.

"Isn't she radiant?" Walter said, admiring his beautiful wife. "She even sported a rather provocative bikini when we were there."

"Walter!" she said while playfully patting his face. "I can't believe you said that."

Wow, Bobby thought. This guy has seriously lightened up since that first meeting in the diner. Walter smiled and took Bobby by the elbow.

"Can I speak with you for just a second?"

"Sure," Bobby replied.

"Listen," Walter said. "I never adequately thanked you for all you have done for us."

"That's my job, Walter. That's what you paid me for," Bobby said.

"No, I paid you to follow my wife," Walter said, slightly misty-eyed. "You went well above that. You risked your life to save that little girl and protect Nina. I can't even fathom how someone musters that kind of courage." With that, Walter reached into his breast pocket and produced another thick envelope.

"Walter," Bobby said. "You have already paid me. This isn't necessary. Anyway, I already asked you for a favor."

"Yes, I have made all the arrangements," Walter said, beaming. "This, Robert Luca Bocchini, is what we call a performance bonus, and I won't take no for an answer." He pressed the envelope into Bobby's hand. Bobby took the envelope, which felt even heavier than the first one, and placed it in his jacket pocket.

"Thank you, Walter!" Bobby said.

"No, Bobby. Thank you!" He turned on his heels and headed back to his lovely wife.

"What was that all about?" asked Autumn.

Bobby smiled. "It was an unexpected windfall. Tell me, Autumn, have you ever been to the Virgin Islands?"

"No," she said, "I've never really been anywhere."

"I suggest you get a passport. We are taking a brief vacation!" he said and kissed her.

Ten minutes later, the guests of honor arrived, albeit quietly, almost covertly, through the back service door. The coverage and fervor surrounding Jessica and her story had not yet abated. They were welcomed by a hush followed by a roar of applause from a gathering of about sixty friends, relatives, and neighbors as they walked into the room. One person who was notably absent was Jessica's mother. Thomas called her to let her know they had found Jessica. Jessica had spoken to her on the phone, but she hadn't visited her yet. Thomas explained to Bobby that his ex-wife hadn't fared well in the years since Jessica's abduction. Jessica's return intensified her self-loathing despite her frequent therapy sessions. It would be a process, but he felt sure they would eventually get together. They had arranged a lavish dinner for the event. Aunt Gina's cook and wait staff collaborated with Ernie and Darla to create a four-course sit-down dinner. Bobby was sitting at a large round table with his family, Autumn, and, naturally, his mother. The staff removed the appetizer and salad courses, and people chatted and laughed. Bobby's eyes widened in horror when the wait staff placed the main course in front of him. Besides a wonderful veal cutlet, there was pasta, but not just any. It was Ernie's fettuccine Alfredo! Bobby could feel his mother's stare boring into his skull. He glanced up and smiled. She did not return the smile. She simply glared at him; her look seemed to say, go ahead, take a fork full, you traitor!

"Oh, it's the fettuccine you like," Autumn said. Bobby glanced at her, his eyes pleading.

Ernie stopped by the table. "What a wonderful evening! Is everyone enjoying their dinner?"

Sal could sense the tension at the table and knew the background story of the fettuccine incident. So, he tried to diffuse the situation. "Everything is wonderful, Ernie; the veal is succulent."

Ernie smiled and said, "I chose the pasta Alfredo for you, Bobby, since you seemed to like it at the diner."

Bobby's brother Tony couldn't help himself. "Yeah, Bobby said it was the best fettuccine Alfredo he had ever had." His brother looked at him and snickered safely from across the table.

Bobby began to say something when Sal interrupted, "He told me it was one of the best, but like all good Italian sons, Ernie, his mother's sauce is still number one. You understand."

"Absolutely!" Ernie said. "But Mrs. Bocchini, would you honor me by telling me about your thoughts on it?" Ernie asked. "Or how I might improve on it."

Bobby's mother spun the pasta on her fork and took a bite. The entire table waited with all eyes on her.

"Ernesto," she said, "Are you sure your mother wasn't Italian? It's wonderful; we can compare recipes sometime."

Ernie beamed, and Bobby let out a long exhale and dug into his dinner. His mother was right; it was wonderful. He would, of course, torture his little brother later. He shot his mother another glance, and she gave him a thin smile and shook her finger at him.

FIFTY:
_____

FAVOR

As the evening was winding down, Bobby introduced Thomas Grant to Walter. "Thomas, do you know Walter Adams?" he asked.

"Well, only by reputation," Thomas said as the two shook hands. When the Grants returned from their staycation, the reality of their situation became very clear. Thomas had gone bankrupt and lost nearly everything in his quest to find Jessica. He now lived in a cramped and run-down studio apartment in a not-so-desirable part of town. Jessica was held captive for years in a tiny space, and was just happy to be back home. She didn't care about the location of the home. Being with her dad was the only thing that mattered. Thomas wanted the best for his little girl, as any good father would. He even considered asking his ex-wife to let Jessica stay with her until he was back on his feet. It brought Jessica to tears at the thought. All of this was not lost on Bobby. He made Walter aware of the situation and asked Walter to help.

"Thomas, I am so thrilled to see you and Jessica reunited!" Walter began. "Have you given any thought to what's next?"

Thomas shook his head and ran his hands through his thinning gray hair. "To be honest, Mr. Adams—"

"Please call me Walter," he said with a smile.

"Walter," Thomas corrected. "The past few weeks have my head spinning. I'm afraid I haven't even thought about it."

Walter nodded. "That is totally understandable. Well, allow me to give you something to consider. You did excellent work as a fund manager before, and it so happens I have an open position."

Thomas frowned a bit. "Walter, that's very kind, but I have been out of the game for years, and I don't want to become some kind of charity case."

"Good, that's not what I'm offering," Walter clarified. "Our company was recently awarded a contract to manage a large retirement fund for a group of schoolteachers from the Midwest. The goal is to increase their pension monies and hedge against inflation. It's not as challenging as what you're accustomed to, but I have faith in your abilities. If we can build a solid reputation, it could turn into a new operating unit for us. What do you say?"

Thomas was trying to wrap his head around the offer. But before he could, Walter doubled down, "Oh, I almost forgot. Besides a six-figure salary and benefits, it also comes with a two-bedroom apartment in our building. We used to use it as an added perk for our interns and junior executives, but in the post-Covid world, they would rather work remotely." Bobby held his breath. "Well, what do you say?" Walter asked as Nina joined the group.

Thomas glanced at Jessica across the room. As tears filled his eyes, he emphatically said, "Yes!"

"That's fantastic!" Nina said, and the entire group cheered. Jessica, who had been under the watchful eyes and protection of Sal, Diane Battle, and the entire Bocchini clan, joined the group.

Thomas hugged his little girl. "Jessica, Dad has a new job, and we have a place to live!"

Bobby said, "Let's drink a toast to that!" The group strolled to the bar. The staff poured glasses of champagne. Bobby smiled at Walter and Nina. Walter winked at Bobby.

Thomas Grant pulled Bobby aside. "Mr. Bocchini," he said, "I'm not an idiot. I know you had a hand in all this," Bobby protested, but Thomas stopped him. "Don't deny it. Thank you. I do not know how, but someday I will repay you."

Bobby smiled. "Just go hug your little girl. That's more than enough payment for me." Thomas headed to the bar. "

"Are three miracles required for sainthood?" Sal asked Getz. Bobby gave both men the bird.

"Saints don't behave like that," Getz said. "Anyway, he's too chubby to be a saint."

Bobby shook his head. "Everyone is a comedian tonight!"

FIFTY-ONE:

LEVERAGE IS A FUNNY THING

The scene at the Brooklyn Metropolitan Detention Center was a little less jovial. Valon Koci had gone before the judge. They charged him with sex trafficking and later with the murder of Orik Selmani, an Armenian national. The FBI and police found him sitting in a chair near the fireplace. Selmani's lifeless body was sitting across from him. The murder weapon was on the floor beside Koci. Gun residue on his hands, which were above his head, his high-priced attorney pleaded not guilty on his behalf. Koci said nothing, nothing to the police, nothing at the arraignment. He didn't have to say anything. His attorney possessed certain files and documents. The files contained a detailed list of high-profile individuals, including celebrities, businessmen, politicians, and even a judge. Koci had bet his life that it would be enough to keep him from facing prosecution or prison. He had an elaborate escape plan ready once he got released on bail. There was a certain cargo container waiting at the port of Baltimore, a short three-hour drive. They had retrofitted the container as a cozy apartment with heat, a restroom, and supplies for the six-day sail to Port Puerto Isabel in Nicaragua. He wasn't looking forward to the 2139 nautical mile trip, but Nicaragua had no extradition agreement with the US. From there, he would make his way back to Mexico; he owned the local police and judges there. This had been a setback for him, sure, but nothing he couldn't overcome. Koci still had an extensive network of similar business concerns around the world. He would set up shop again in Mexico, then identify and eliminate the traitor who brought the FBI to his door and the woman Selmani referred to. Then he would watch with delight as the information on all those famous perverts made its way to the media. The thought of the coming carnage made him smile. He fell asleep without realizing he had badly overplayed his hand. These same powerful people couldn't risk him making it to a courtroom. He was also unaware that, at that very moment, they had killed his attorney in a puzzling home invasion. The police followed up on a disturbance complaint and found the attorney dead. Detectives believed the hole in the wall behind the attorney's desk had contained a safe, but could not find it or its contents. The medical examiner stated in his autopsy report that someone had severed several fingers of the attorney with a bolt cutter. The neighbors said they had heard men speaking what sounded like Russian. Koci knew none of this as he drifted off to sleep. Something woke him sometime around 2 am. Two figures entered his cell. He attempted to yell, but they silenced him immediately. The captors quickly made his bed sheets into a noose, tied it around his neck and gagged him. The sheets looped over the top bars of the cell, and they hoisted him aloft.

They found his lifeless body the next morning as breakfast was being delivered. Investigators also found a gap in surveillance footage during the incident. Certain powerful men quickly dismissed those concerns, with much to lose. Valon Koci, conveniently, had committed suicide. No one would lose sleep over that.

Michael Brady was the federal witness against Valon Koci and his organization. A witness was no longer necessary. Suddenly, he, too, became a liability. The authorities quickly charged Brady with the kidnapping of Jessica Grant and sex trafficking. He would however never make it to trial. It seemed a mysterious clerical error had caused him to be moved from protective custody to the general population. He didn't last a day. An inmate serving three consecutive life sentences shoved an ice pick or something similar into his left ear and stabbed him three times in his heart. Even the most hardened murderers and criminals maintained a special contempt for those who harmed children.

FIFTY-TWO

SUNSET

On a sun-drenched beach just off Red Hook Bay in the US Virgin Island of St. Thomas, Bobby Bocchini was relaxing in the sun. He and Autumn had checked into the Limetree Beach Resort almost a week ago. They had experienced breathtaking views from the harbor in Charlotte Amalie and the comfort of their hotel. Their room had a stunning view of the Caribbean beach and the crystal blue waters. They had wonderful dinners, explored, and shopped duty-free in the local markets. They even tried snorkeling at Sapphire Beach. Even though it was January, the temperature was a perfect eighty-three degrees.

Bobby noticed New York had just had a snowstorm. He couldn't resist texting his brother Anthony a picture of him and Autumn on the beach relaxing with a couple of Piña coladas. He added, "Have a wonderful time shoveling the driveway, numb nuts!"

The couple had grown closer and Bobby's feelings for her were undeniable. Autumn had helped Bobby manage the flood and interview requests and the tidal wave of new business that had come from the Jessica Grant case. She also encouraged him to start his physical therapy again and to add intermittent fasting. Bobby shed around 20 pounds. His limp remained, but it was now only slight. He no longer used a cane to walk.

On the last evening of their vacation, they were on a catamaran sunset cruise. As Bobby gazed at Autumn, her auburn hair blowing in the breeze, he knelt and produced an engagement ring from his pocket. "Autumn, you are the most wonderful woman I have ever met. I can't even imagine living the rest of my life without you by my side. Will you marry me?" The twenty other passengers collectively held their breath, waiting for her response.

With tears in her eyes, she knelt and said, "Yes, Bobby, I will gladly marry you!" The passengers and crew roared their approval while the sun set in the distance.

THE END